Dolphin Luck

Everly ♥
love Kitty

Dolphin Luck

Hilary McKay

SCHOLASTIC INC.

New York   Toronto   London   Auckland   Sydney
Mexico City   New Delhi   Hong Kong   Buenos Aires

To Margaret
with love from Hilary

ISBN 0-439-38854-6

Copyright © 1998 by Hilary McKay.
All rights reserved.
Published by Scholastic Inc., 555 Broadway, New York, NY 10012,
by arrangement with Aladdin Paperbacks,
an imprint of Simon & Schuster Children's Publishing Division.
SCHOLASTIC and associated logos are trademarks and/or
registered trademarks of Scholastic Inc.

12 11 10 9 8 7 6 5 4 3 2   5 6 7/0

Printed in the U.S.A.   40

First Scholastic printing, February 2002

The text for this book was set in Garamond 3.

Book design by Angela Carlino

one
......

Perry distributed his Christmas cards on the last day before the holiday, twenty of them, all the same, in blank envelopes so as to cut down on delivery time. It was the fashion among seventh-year boys to be very, very casual about Christmas cards: they were ripped open, glanced at, and unsentimentally tossed in the wastebasket in a matter of seconds. Perry chucked one onto the teacher's desk, handed the rest out to the nineteen people nearest to him, and was about to saunter off when he happened to notice that he was being given some curious glances.

"What's up?" he asked Dan, who was standing next to him.

"Nothing," said Dan, dropping his card into the basket. "Cheers, mate! Very nice!"

"Very," agreed Robin, Perry's best friend, and he looked admiringly at the design again, a parade of turkeys marching under the headline TURKEYS ARE REVOLTING. The turkeys carried banners exhorting people to eat robin

1

at Christmas: SLIMMING, TRADITIONAL, AND CHEAP. Perry, with Robin in mind, had invested in two packages of the cards and considered them to be hilarious.

People were certainly smiling.

"Give it back a second!" said Perry to Robin with sudden suspicion.

"Why?" Robin—who, unlike nearly everyone else, made no secret of the fact that he took his Christmas cards home—paused in the act of stuffing it into his pocket.

"Just do . . . Oh no!"

Inside, above where Perry had laconically scrawled his name, someone had carefully written:

With lots of love

and, underneath the signature had been added:

and Sun Dance

and as if that was not bad enough, the bottom of the card had been decorated with a neat row of kisses.

"Bloody Sun Dance!" howled Perry.

"What does it matter?" asked Robin, who, living next door to Perry, knew and understood Perry's younger brother, Sun Dance, completely.

"Are they all like that?" moaned Perry, and after a brief inspection of the wastebasket discovered that they were.

"I'm sure he wasn't meaning to be funny," said Robin.

"That's just it," said Perry. "It wouldn't matter half as much if he was. What must people think?" he added bitterly.

Sun Dance was ten years old, two years younger than Perry and Ant, two years older than his sister Beany. They were the Robinson children, and they lived in one half of

Porridge Hall, an old Victorian house that stood alone on the road out of town and faced the sea of the Yorkshire coast in England. In the other half lived Robin Brogan and his mother; Robin's dog, Friday; and, in season, Mrs. Brogan's bed-and-breakfast guests.

"Who are a mixed blessing," Mrs. Brogan often remarked to Mrs. Robinson. Mrs. Brogan and Mrs. Robinson were very good friends.

"There is no one else I would trust with Sun Dance," Mrs. Robinson said of Mrs. Brogan. Sun Dance—the unpredictable and innocent, with his sparkle and his darkness, his nightmares and his courage and his incomprehensible logic—needed handling with care. Always, always, ever since he had been able to speak, Sun Dance had needed handling with care. He was explained by his parents, shielded by his brother and sisters, and defused, when necessary, like a self-destructing bomb. Always, always, always.

In the past Perry had understood this, fought Sun Dance's battles and forgiven his excesses. It was bad enough being Sun Dance, Perry had understood, without having it chucked in your face, and Perry's parents had said,"The children are wonderful with Sun Dance. Perry is marvelous. I don't know what he would do without Perry."

Lately Perry had grown sick of being marvelous, and his patience had begun to run out.

"What did you *do* it for?" he yelled, marching into where his sisters and brother were peacefully watching TV and hurling Robin's card in front of Sun Dance.

"To help," said Sun Dance.

Perry had known that already. He had remembered

Sun Dance watching him scribble his Christmas cards the night before and asking, "Is that all you're going to put?" and showing him his own carefully written pile.

"I couldn't write all that rubbish," he had said to Sun Dance. "It would take all night."

So Sun Dance had done it for him.

"Were people pleased?" asked Sun Dance. "Did people say how neat I'd done it? Were they glad I put my name too?"

"Kisses!" shouted Perry. "What do you think people *thought?* Lots of love! *Lots of love!* And putting your name and calling yourself Sun Dance!"

This last criticism surprised even Perry; he didn't know why he had said it. Nobody, including himself, had called Sun Dance anything else for years and years. Nevertheless, he continued ruthlessly with his tirade. "And it's about time everyone stopped calling him that! He's got a perfectly good name of his own!"

"What, me? I've got a perfectly good name of my own?" asked Sun Dance after a tiny moment's pause during which everyone strove to remind themselves of what his name actually was.

"Yes, so stop pretending you've forgotten!"

"Forgotten what?"

"It was only ever a game, calling you Sun Dance."

"You and Ant were Butch and Cassidy," said Sun Dance slowly, "and I was Sun Dance. Because you said I was old enough to play." Sun Dance tugged off his glasses and scrubbed his eyes. "You said I was Sun Dance and I *am* Sun Dance!"

"You're not," said Perry.

There was a very nasty silence. Nobody looked at Perry. Nobody said he was quite right. He reached out and drew Old Blanket, the family dog, toward him as a shield and ally, and from Old Blanket there came a revolting noise and a fresh and terrible smell.

"*Darling* Old Blanket," said Ant.

"I shan't stop being Beany," said Beany, who had once expressed a yearning for the quiet life of a bean. "I shan't be Elizabeth again, whatever you say."

"It doesn't matter about you," growled Perry. "At least you *know*."

"Know what?"

"Who you're supposed to be."

"Sun Dance knows who he's supposed to be, don't you, Sun Dance," said Ant.

"Yes," said Sun Dance uncertainly.

Late that night the wind began to rise. In the house Mrs. Robinson coughed and Old Blanket groaned, his hind leg thumping the floor as he scratched. From the kitchen came the distant rumble of the tumble dryer. Perry, on the top bunk in the room he shared with Sun Dance, sprawled and murmured, comforted by sleep, safe in a world where it didn't matter what anyone thought, where it was not necessary to toss away your Christmas cards and be tough and cool, tougher and cooler than anyone else because your kid brother was so different from everyone else's kid brothers. "Off the rails," somebody had said, describing Sun Dance that afternoon, but in his dreams Perry had forgotten.

Sun Dance lay awake remembering. First he had been

a baby. After that he had begun; he had been a person, but a person too young to play. Perry and Ant, who were twins, had seemed far away, out of reach. Then, one glorious day, Perry had said he was no longer too young and had told him he was Sun Dance, and he had been Sun Dance ever since. And now Perry, who had given him his name, had taken it away, and was once again drifting out of reach.

Perry's most uncharacteristic outburst of nastiness seemed to leave no visible trace at all. Beany and Ant never referred to it. Sun Dance continued to answer to his name, just as he had always done. Perry, away from the pressure of school, appeared to revert to his old pigheaded, optimistic self, but occasionally an expression on Sun Dance's face would cause him to experience vague murmurings of guilt, as if he had perpetrated some shabby, undiscovered deed. This caused him to treat Sun Dance with a slightly reserved gentleness. Sun Dance noticed this and was not at all grateful. He far preferred being yelled at, but it seemed he had no choice. The gap between himself and Perry was widening and widening; he could not imagine how he would ever catch up with him again.

There were other worries in those days before Christmas: Mrs. Robinson's way of catching her chest when she coughed; the weather, which was horrible without being exciting; and something nameless that seemed to shadow Old Blanket and caused the children to love him more than ever and the adults to avoid each other's eyes.

* * *

"It's not very Christmassy," remarked B
lately on Christmas Eve. "We need something
happen."

"Christmas will happen tomorrow," said Mrs. Brogan.

"Something beside that. Something special."

"What sort of special?"

"Something lucky. We need some luck," said Beany.

two
· · · · · ·

The Robinsons were spending Christmas Eve next door
with Robin and his mother. Mrs. Robinson had gone to
bed.

"Gone to bed in *daytime!*" Sun Dance told Mrs. Brogan. *"On Christmas Eve!"*

"No wonder it doesn't feel Christmassy," said Ant.

"The weather doesn't help," remarked Perry. "It's hard
to stop listening to it."

"We really *do* need some luck," said Beany again.

"Tell them a story," Robin urged his mother. "Tell
them about the dolphin sword. It was terrible weather
then, wasn't it?"

"Yes, and they needed luck if anyone did," agreed his
mother.

"That's what reminded me."

"Go on, tell us then," said Perry, so Mrs. Brogan,
who was always happy to oblige with a story, began at
once.

"All week—"

"It's a Viking story," interrupted Robin. "You ought to tell them it's a Viking story before you begin."

"It's a Viking story," said Mrs. Brogan, and began again.

"All week there had been terrible weather off the Yorkshire coast, and the last day of the journey was the worst. They had had a dreadful time, and it had been worst of all for Freya, who had been sick ever since the first wave lifted her father's wooden ship from the shingle beach of home. Already she had lost count of how many days ago that had been.

"'A few,' said her father with aggravating cheerfulness, so Freya did not ask again. Her father never would admit that anything was worse than he expected, but when he looked up at the racing clouds and remarked that things were not so bad, then Freya knew that they were very bad indeed.

"The wind and sea battled all around them. They were miles off course and caught in a storm, Freya and her three elder brothers and her father and all they possessed in the world. Freya's voice was shriller than the yowling wind. 'I want to go home!' she wailed.

("Freya never had been very good at putting up with things," explained Mrs. Brogan.)

"'It isn't fair,' Freya sobbed. 'I want to go home! I shall die and then you'll be sorry! I'm so tired, tired, tired!'

"'Go to sleep then,' said her father.

"Freya gave him one glance of astonishment and reproach, dropped her sodden head onto a pile of sodden bedding, and went to sleep.

"When she woke up, there was something lying across her lap. It was her father's sword. His precious sword with the dolphin-shaped hilt that no one was ever allowed to touch. There was a story in the family that when the roof of the homestead had blazed up, Freya's father had rushed inside and grabbed first the baby (who was Freya) and then his sword. And after that the boys. The sword was beautiful and mysterious. It had even been known to grant wishes.

"'Dolphin luck,' said the family whenever this happened. It was a sword of good fortune.

"'Hold tight to that,' said Freya's father.

"Freya held very tight and screwed shut her eyes and ducked her head against the spray-soaked wind and wished: 'I wish we could land safe out of this horrible boat, I wish we could land safe out of this horrible boat, I wish we could land safe out of this horrible boat.'"

Mrs. Brogan had told the story of the Viking ship that came ashore in the little bay opposite Porridge Hall many times before. It was part of winter—Robin had heard it half a dozen times at least—but to the Robinsons it was entirely new.

"And were they wrecked?" demanded Perry eagerly. "Or saved?"

"Saved," said Mrs. Brogan.

"All of them?"

"Everyone. And the dog."

"Had they brought a dog?" asked Ant, who could hardly have borne to listen to the story if she had known there was a dog on board.

Robin grinned across at his mother, knowing quite well that the dog had been added solely for the benefit of their next-door neighbors.

"Do you think Freya would have let them leave their dog behind?" replied Mrs. Brogan.

"How do you know her name was Freya?" asked Beany.

"Freya is a nice name," said Mrs. Brogan.

"And what happened to the dolphin sword?" demanded Sun Dance.

"Freya dropped it."

"Dropped it!"

"Right at the last minute."

There was a moment of silence.

"Wasn't Freya's father furious?" Perry wondered out loud.

"He was never furious with Freya," said Mrs. Brogan. "Perhaps if it had been one of the boys . . . No, I don't think he would have been angry even with the boys. I expect he was just glad to have them safely ashore. And the dolphin sword did what he wanted it to do; gave Freya something to hang on to for the last bit of the journey. It really *was* terrible weather."

"It is now," said Robin. "Listen to the wind!"

The wind was almost frightening. It hooted and echoed across the chimneys and clutched at the curtains. It hurled horizontal lines of icy rain at the windowpanes with a noise like stones. It had whipped the waves into a churning frenzy. It was as salty as the sea.

"My poor garden!" said Mrs. Brogan. "My poor, poor roses!"

"The lights are flickering again," said Perry. The power and telephone lines had been down over and over again. "Dad says if they come down over Christmas, they'll leave them down."

"Rubbish!" said Mrs. Brogan robustly.

"Christmas trees just aren't the same without proper fairy lights," said Ant.

"I think they're better," said Sun Dance. "More exciting. Could that sword really grant wishes?"

"Well, that's the story," said Mrs. Brogan. "Dolphin luck, it was called. What would you wish for yourselves?"

"I would wish for a puppy," Ant, who had been sharing the hearth rug with Robin's dog, Friday, answered before anyone else could speak. "Old Blanket is getting so old. He won't play anymore and he growls when you try."

"I would wish for a million wishes," said Perry.

"That's cheating!" said Ant at once.

"I would still do it."

"You would soon get tired of it then," said Mrs. Brogan. "What about you, Beany?"

"Mum to be better," said Beany, and all the cheerfulness that Mrs. Brogan and Robin had worked so hard to create disappeared as if it had never been. No matter how bright the fire, nor how fragrant the roasting chestnuts, nobody could forget for more than a few minutes how ill Mrs. Robinson had become. She had been poorly for days and it felt like weeks. Her illness had made Mr. Robinson short-tempered with worry, Beany and Ant mournful, and Sun Dance even more remote and distracted than usual.

Perry sighed irritably at the reminder. Illness in the house made him feel as angry and helpless as an animal caught in a trap.

"Come on! Cheer up!" said Mrs. Brogan, handing Perry the chestnut roaster and hugging Beany. "It's only a bad dose of flu she's got. She's having a nasty time of it, poor thing, but it will soon be over. Whatever are you finding to look at out there, Sun Dance?"

Sun Dance, not listening as usual, was peering out through the black, streaming windows.

"It must still be there," they heard him murmur.

"What must still be there?" asked Robin, and Sun Dance shook himself like a dog coming out of water, came back to the present, and replied, "The dolphin sword."

"It was found once," said Mrs. Brogan. "Found and then lost again, at least that's the story I was told when I was a little girl. How are those chestnuts getting on? Tip them onto the hearth to cool for a while, Perry. I'm afraid that will have to be the last batch. I heard your front door slam a minute ago; your father must be on his way. Save him a few chestnuts, won't you?"

"He doesn't like roasted chestnuts," said Ant. "He says they're indigestible."

"Rotten old Dad!" remarked Sun Dance. "It wouldn't matter half as much if it was him that was ill!"

"Sun Dance!" exclaimed Mrs. Brogan, laughing. "What a heartless remark!"

"It isn't," argued Sun Dance. "It's just true. Mum always says he *enjoys* being ill . . ."

There was a knock on the living-room door at that moment and Mr. Robinson's face peered around.

"Come in! Come in!" cried Mrs. Brogan. "Never mind the drips!"

"I shouldn't really," said Mr. Robinson wearily, but he entered anyway, looking extremely harassed and as drenched as if he had just crawled out of the sea.

"You never got that soaked just coming across the gardens?" exclaimed Robin.

"How right you are!" Mr. Robinson shook his wet hair out of his eyes and huffed on his fingers. "I've been down on the beach shouting at that bloo . . . that bla . . . that *idiot* dog of ours for the last half hour! Now don't start wailing at me, Ant! Nobody made him go out; it was his own decision! He slipped past me while I was trying to fix the mailbox so that the rain wouldn't blow in, and I'd just discovered your mother had been standing on the doorstep in all this wind calling for him—"

"How is she?" interrupted Mrs. Brogan.

"More or less the same, thanks," replied Mr. Robinson, stooping down to pour a pile of presents under the Christmas tree. "She said thank you very much for having them all this afternoon and have a Happy Christmas and not to worry. You've got people coming for the day, haven't you?"

"Only Robin's friend Dan and his mother and father," replied Mrs. Brogan. "So if you need anything, anything at all, you only have to say! And tell her she's sent far too much! All those parcels!"

"That's what she said about you!"

"There's never too much Christmas," said Robin.

"And Old Blanket's bound to be back soon. He's still got some sense left."

"Of course he has," said Mrs. Brogan cheerfully.

It was very quiet when the Robinsons had gone home. Robin always loved Christmas Eve, the long day of tingling excitement that followed his birthday on the twenty-third.

"I am twelve and a day," he thought, and felt perfectly happy.

In the house next door, things were far from happy. Swords of good fortune, Viking ships, the storm outside, and Mrs. Robinson's flu all temporarily faded into insignificance. Old Blanket was missing and quite suddenly nothing else mattered.

"He could have had an accident and be lying somewhere paralyzed and stuck," said Ant with tears in her eyes. "Like that time he got his head trapped in Mrs. Brogan's fridge and nearly choked to death."

"Perhaps he went down to the beach and a wave swept him away," suggested Perry.

"He never goes near the waves," said Mr. Robinson crossly. "Please don't start making things worse than they are."

"Or went onto the cliff path and got blown off."

"We should be so lucky!" muttered Mr. Robinson, and was overheard.

"Dad!"

"Well you must admit that it's highly unlikely! Too low slung for a start!"

"Perhaps somebody drove past and kidnapped him!"

"Who would want him?" asked Mr. Robinson, losing patience. "The great, smelly, stupid, thumping nuisance!"

"He's run away, I know he has," said Ant.

"Of course he hasn't run away," wheezed Mrs. Robinson, coming into the room at that moment. "Go and look through the house again. He might have slipped back in and be hiding somewhere."

"He'd be all wet," said Ant miserably. "And I've been upstairs and checked the quilts, and they're all still on the beds."

Everyone knew what she meant. Old Blanket, in his declining years, had developed a hatred of wetness, and although no longer agile enough to climb onto the beds, had resourcefully learned to dry himself by pulling off the quilts with his teeth and rolling on them. He had done it only the day before.

"He's run away because you smacked him for it," Ant told her mother reproachfully.

"It's never bothered him in the past!" replied her mother. "Oh, my head does feel dreadful! I shall have to go back to bed or I'll be fit for nothing tomorrow. Is nobody going to hang up the Christmas stockings?"

"How can we possibly have Christmas without Old Blanket?" asked Ant.

It was very late before anyone went to bed that night. It was very nearly Christmas day.

"Can't we stop the clocks?" asked Sun Dance desperately.

Mr. Robinson said stopping the clocks was not an option. Nor would he agree to calling the police. He heartlessly forced them all upstairs, and the only concessions he would make were that all the lights should be left on, the front door propped open a crack (since the storm was dying out at last), and that he himself would wait up for the wanderer and see that he was given hot milk and supper the moment he arrived.

"And will you come straight upstairs and wake us up and tell us?" asked Ant hopefully.

"NO, I WILL *NOT!*" shouted Mr. Robinson.

The Christmas presents fell rather flat that year. They began with Sun Dance's, small packs of jellybeans for everyone except Perry, to whom Sun Dance rather nervously offered an enormous Scotch tape–covered package. A great deal of worry had gone into Perry's present. Sun Dance desperately hoped that it would make things better again. Perry, he thought, must either roar with laughter and say it was horrible (and then everything would be all right) or pour scorn completely and say it was horrible (and then they could have a proper, refreshing fight and afterward things would be all right). The first alternative would be best, but either would be an improvement.

"You used to say you'd like a real one," he said as he handed it over. "It *looks* real!"

It did look real. It was a hideously painted, six-foot squirming rubber snake.

"How perfectly revolting," said Mrs. Robinson.

"It's very nice," said Perry politely. "Very nice indeed. Thank you."

After that the unwrapping just got worse.

Ever since the Robinson children had stopped believing in Father Christmas, there had been a family tradition concerning the most expensive, most exciting, most longed-for Christmas presents. It was that they were given by Old Blanket. They were always wrapped in empty dog-food bags with paw-printy labels that read:

Love from Old Blanket

It was almost better than believing in Father Christmas, believing in Old Blanket. The whole family vied with each other in telling stories of how their faithful and noble dog begged and earned the necessary money, staggered into town with it clutched in his teeth, purchased his Christmas presents (often with great suffering and ingenuity), and, exhausted but content, carried them home and wrapped them in his empty dog-food bags. It was a good sort of joke usually—that was, when Old Blanket was on hand to smirk complacently over the unwrapping, to be hugged and cuddled and generally adored. It was not a good joke at all when he was missing. On Christmas morning the unwrapping became more and more dismal as Old Blanket's offerings (prepared weeks before by Mrs. Robinson and forgotten until it was too late to do anything about them) were openly sobbed over by their receivers.

"This is absolutely ridiculous!" said Mr. Robinson. "And if I'd had my way it would never have come to it! That dog should have been at the vet's months ago when he first started snapping at people!"

"Well, I hope you feel guilty!" said Ant, when it was discovered a few minutes later that Old Blanket had selflessly bought Mr. Robinson a very expensive German lens for his camera.

"No, I *don't!*" said Mr. Robinson, and stamped off to shut himself in the kitchen to finish preparing dinner. He was the sort of man who could not cook unless he had absolute privacy and silence, which, Mrs. Robinson sometimes remarked, was all very well.

"If that dog comes back," he promised himself as he turned up the oven to give the turkey a final browning, "I shall wait until the children go back to school . . ." (He added cream to the bread sauce, stirred it carefully, ground in black pepper, tasted it, paused to consider, and added two drops of lemon juice and an invisible quantity of salt.) "Yes, I'll wait until they're back at school and then I shall telephone that vet myself (those potatoes are done and so are the sprouts; another sixty seconds perhaps, for utter perfection), explain about his bad temper and the dreadful smell that *does* exist—it is not my imagination, whatever the children say (that gravy is perfect, a bay leaf makes all the difference). After all he is fourteen at least and quite possibly more . . . (That sauce could be warmer and gravy should always be boiling hot. It is a well-known fact that all the best cooks are men. Attention to detail and absolutely *critical* timing, that's what it comes down to! Colander.) Yes, I shall explain to the vet about his age (colander, colander, colander—damn thing's vanished) and suggest that it would be doing the dog a kindness . . . WHAT ON EARTH IS THAT TERRIBLE STENCH?"

It was more than a year since Old Blanket had been thin enough to squeeze through the enormous cat flap that had been cut for him in the kitchen door, but he appeared to have forgotten this fact.

"It simply isn't fair," moaned Mr. Robinson.

Old Blanket was sodden and snarling and appeared to have swollen to twice his usual size. It took Perry and his father more than half an hour to extract him from the kitchen door, the whole operation having to be performed from behind in the rain because of the ominous growls that poured from his chest throughout the rescue.

"Poor, poor darling!" said Ant.

"He smells a bit," said Perry.

"He smells an awful lot," said Beany, who always told the truth. "He's been rolling in washed-up dead seagulls again."

"He eats them too," remarked Sun Dance, "so I think Old Blanket is very brave. When is it dinnertime?"

Mr. Robinson, who had been quietly beating his head against the kitchen wall, suddenly stiffened and made a dash for the stove, but his wife got there before him.

"You can't possibly touch anything before you've had a bath," she ordered, "and neither can Perry! You're both covered in . . . in . . . well, whatever Old Blanket's been rolling in! Ant, don't you dare go near that dog! Put some sausages in his dish and put him out on the porch; he will have to be scrubbed, but I can't face it at the moment. Beany, get your father a drink. Whiskey. He won't want anything in it. Take it up to him, Sun Dance, and tell him I am rescuing the dinner . . ."

* * *

Despite Mrs. Robinson's valiant efforts, dinner was beyond rescue. The turkey had browned to a point that could only be described as black, the bread sauce and gravy had turned to glue, and the vegetables had boiled to soup. And when dinner was over, the dreadful ordeal of scrubbing Old Blanket had to be faced. It was done in the garden with a hose and a bucket full of dog shampoo. Mr. Robinson was restrained with difficulty from using bleach.

After Old Blanket had been scrubbed, he was shut in the kitchen to dry. While he was there, he ate the whole of the remains of the turkey and a box of rum truffles.

The next day, Boxing Day morning, he bit Mr. Robinson for no apparent reason unless it was true, as Ant said defensively, that he sensed Mr. Robinson had stopped loving him.

On Boxing Day afternoon he crawled under Mr. and Mrs. Robinson's bed and was terribly sick.

"Food poisoning," said Ant, scowling at her father's bandaged hand.

On Boxing Day evening he died.

Ant's tearful request that Old Blanket might spend one last night in her bedroom was turned down by her flinty-hearted father.

"But I don't want him to be buried yet," she sobbed.

"He has to be buried if he's dead," said Sun Dance, who had moments of surprising reasonableness. "And Dad is digging him a lovely enormous grave."

The grave was to be at the very bottom of the garden. Mr. Robinson, in an ancient duffle coat and rubber boots, had braved the darkness and wind and begun it the moment Old Blanket had been pronounced dead. He had been outside for ages, digging by the light of a hurricane lamp with a bottle of whiskey propped handily within reach. Occasionally he broke into song.

"He's promised to put in the waterproof picnic rug for him to lie on, " said Beany. "And wrap him in his blanket with his favorite sofa cushion, and his bowl, and a Mars bar from my selection box, and the rest of his bag of biscuits, and a can of dog food. And a can opener of course."

"Dogs can't use can openers," objected Perry. "And it does seem a waste to bury him. Goodness knows when Dad will let us have another dog. I don't see why he can't just be stuffed."

"The trouble with stuffing," said Sun Dance dreamily, "is that they must have to have their insides taken out first . . ."

"Shut up! Shut up!" said Ant.

"Yes, shut up!" agreed Beany. "Stuffing wouldn't be nice at all, and of course he'll be able to use a can opener. He'll be in heaven, won't he?"

"My guinea pig didn't go to heaven," said Sun Dance. "I dug him up to see if he had, and he was still there. More or less."

"Your guinea pig had never done anything *good* to get to heaven," pointed out Beany.

"He'd never done anything bad either."

"Well then," said Beany reasonably. "If he'd never done anything good and never done anything bad, where did you expect him to go? No wonder he stayed where he was!"

"Old Blanket was always good," said Sun Dance. "Nearly."

"No, always, always," said Ant, weeping again at the memory of Old Blanket's goodness.

"What about running away on Christmas Eve and rolling on those seagulls and biting Dad and eating the turkey?" asked Perry.

"He must have been very, very poorly," said Ant. "Poorly, and we didn't realize, not bad. I wish we didn't have to wonder. I wish we *knew* Old Blanket would go to heaven."

"Easy enough to find out," said Perry. "When the weather gets a bit warmer and Mum and Dad are out of the way . . ."

Mrs. Robinson, who had spent the day in bed tossing with fever, crawled downstairs in time to catch the tail end of this conversation. Even after night had fallen and Old Blanket (plus the enormous pile of equipment considered necessary for his afterlife) had been laid to rest, it went through and through her mind.

"I cannot bear it," she croaked, staggering out to where Mr. Robinson was happily leveling the grave. "I'm afraid it won't do!"

"What won't do?" asked Mr. Robinson, staring at his wife in amazement. "You shouldn't be out in this freezing wind."

"The children—"

"I thought they were in bed," interrupted Mr. Robinson.

"They are planning to dig him up when the weather gets warmer, and I cannot bear it."

Mr. Robinson gave an enormous groan and hurled his spade at the grave.

"He is a big dog," whispered Mrs. Robinson, with tears pouring down her cheeks, "and when the weather gets warmer . . ."

"Come in at once before you freeze," ordered Mr. Robinson.

"They dig up everything. They always have. I am not at all cold."

Mr. Robinson reached across and felt her hands and then her head, and it was true that she was not cold. She was burning hot.

"What shall we do?" she cried. "They'll dig him up, I know they will!"

"They won't," said Mr. Robinson gently. "I'll make sure they don't. Now come to bed. I'm calling the doctor in the morning."

The doctor said Mrs. Robinson had pneumonia, and Mr. Robinson said bitterly that it was all Old Blanket's fault.

three
●●●●●●●●

"Just look at the sea!" said Sun Dance. "The waves are roaring like lions! Huge white lions in the foam, trying to get to the house. Trying to tear it down!"

This was exactly the sort of Sun Dance remark that usually irritated Perry so much, but this time he showed no sign of having heard at all, not even bothering to point out Sun Dance's probable fate at school should he still be talking such rubbish in a year or so's time. Sun Dance's snow lions were allowed to rage unchallenged. Anyway, they all had much more immediate worries.

"I can't bear to think of tomorrow," groaned Ant, and Beany agreed and Perry said he didn't know why Beany was feeling sorry for herself. Nothing awful was going to happen to *her*.

"But I hate anything awful happening to any of us," said Beany mournfully. "And I hate being left behind, even from awfulness."

Perry said she didn't know what she was talking about.

"I only like things if we do them all together," said Beany.

Perry said she had a brain like a sheep.

"Stop being so horrible to Beany," Ant ordered. "It's not her fault our father is a selfish, cruel, mean, dog-murdering tyrant."

"Not dog-murdering," protested Beany, trying to be fair. "He didn't actually *murder* Old Blanket."

"Old Blanket died of a broken heart and that turkey Dad cooked on Christmas day," retorted Ant. "If that's not murder, I don't know what is, and everything has been horrible ever since."

Nobody argued with that because for nearly two weeks now life in the Robinson family had been more horrible than any of them would have believed possible. It had begun with some truly dreadful days when Mrs. Robinson's pneumonia had been so bad that saintly behavior was all any of them had the heart for, and had been followed by a week when Mrs. Robinson had slowly improved and the saintly behavior had rather broken down. During that time things might have cheered up a bit if Mr. Robinson hadn't talked so constantly about the advantages of boarding school.

After that there had been a weekend when Mrs. Robinson announced that she was completely recovered and had endured enough fussing to last her for the rest of her life. To prove how well she had suddenly become, she recklessly arose from her sick bed and planned and cooked an entire new Christmas dinner to make up for the one that had been ruined, and just as it was almost ready to serve, she collapsed into a quiet heap on the kitchen floor.

This loss of a second turkey seemed to be too much for Mr. Robinson. He prised the gravy spoon from his wife's hand, carted her to the sofa, summoned the doctor, and stood staring bleakly out the window while the diagnosis was made.

"All she needs is a nice, quiet holiday in the sun," said the doctor (who had not been pleased at being disturbed in the middle of his Saturday afternoon). "Madagascar or Barbados. I'll see myself out."

"Madagascar or Barbados!" groaned Mrs. Robinson from the sofa when he had gone. "Oh, he must have been cross! I told you they didn't like being called out on weekends! And another turkey ruined! And why is the house so quiet? Where are the children?"

"I put them outside," said Mr. Robinson heartlessly.

"In the snow? With no dinner?"

"I expect they went straight round next door. I couldn't stand the racket they were making. Nobody could get well in a house like this!"

Mrs. Robinson, resigning herself to the inevitable, lay back and closed her eyes. Her husband's opinions on the possibility of her ever being well again were becoming very familiar. He had recited them so often in the last few days that she almost knew them by heart.

"The weather is utterly appalling!" began Mr. Robinson (as he always did). "If those ridiculous weather forecasters don't come up with something better soon, I shall stop paying attention to them . . ."

"It is hardly their fault," protested Mrs. Robinson.

"They relish it," said her husband bitterly. "They gloat! We've not had a word of apology yet! And then there's the electricity—never on for two hours together—so much for privatization!—and the telephone virtually useless . . ."

"The children?" prompted his wife, so as to get the list over with as soon as possible.

"Biggest nuisance of all!" said Mr. Robinson. "Every day the same! It seems to me that they're only at school for about three seconds, and then they come home starving and shouting and covered in dirty clothes!"

"They always have," interrupted Mrs. Robinson. "You've just never noticed before."

"Ant never shuts up about that miserable dog. Beany is forever under my feet; Sun Dance lives in a world of his own; and Perry is simply a pain!"

"Poor Perry!" said Mrs. Robinson.

"Poor Perry, my foot!" replied Mr. Robinson. "If Perry had to survive one day of the life I lived when I was his age . . ."

"Well, perhaps it will soon be spring," murmured Mrs. Robinson with her eyes closed, but she did not sound very hopeful, and her husband, gazing out at the sodden garden and remembering his own lonely childhood with no family at all except a restless aunt, thought that his children didn't know how lucky they were, and that spring seemed as far off as a dream, and that his wife looked very ill, and that something must be done at once. And finding that the telephone was miraculously working, he began to make calls, first of all to his restless aunt.

* * *

It was the result of these telephone calls that had caused the children to be wrapped in such enormous gloom. Their father appeared to have gone mad in the night.

"I am taking your mother on holiday," he announced that Sunday morning. "Now, nobody say a word until I've finished! On holiday to Barbados. DON'T interrupt! . . . The travel agents had a last-minute cancellation . . . I'M NOT ANSWERING ANY QUESTIONS UNTIL I'VE FINISHED! . . . Mrs. Brogan has said she'll have Sun Dance and Beany to stay with herself and Robin; she'd have had you all, but I told her there was no need—I don't believe in human sacrifice—and the twins' godmother—"

"But . . ." exploded Perry.

"*Please* let me finish!" begged Mr. Robinson desperately. "Your godmother . . ."

"Mad Aunt Mabel!" said Ant incredulously, referring to the restless aunt.

"*Not* mad!" said Mr. Robinson. "Far from mad. Very, very kind in fact—in her own way. Immensely kind in fact! She has said she'll be delighted to have you."

"Mad Aunt Mabel," remarked Perry in accents of extreme patience, "is motorcycling around the world and has been for the last seven years."

"Ah, but she's back," said Mr. Robinson triumphantly. "We had a card at Christmas, and I telephoned her last night before the lines came down again. She is back in Yorkshire and expecting you tomorrow . . . I am not listening to any arguments! I have written and explained the situation to your school . . . IF YOU WAKE YOUR MOTHER, YOU WILL ALL GO STRAIGHT UP TO BED . . . Mrs. Brogan will put Perry and Ant on the train in the afternoon, because we will have left by then, and all you need to do is sit there and you'll be met at the other end. I know it is a shock but tough. For once your mother is coming first. It is only for a week or so, and I promise I'll make it up to you when we get back."

"How?" asked Perry.

"I'm sure you will think of something you want."

"What sort of something?"

"Anything you like," said Mr. Robinson bravely.

From upstairs came the sound of terrible coughing.

"Now is your chance," said Mr. Robinson, "to behave like heroes!"

For the next twenty-four hours the Robinsons did behave like heroes. If their mother had guessed how they really felt, she would never have agreed to leave them, but never for a moment was she allowed to suspect. She was almost hurt.

"They can't wait to get rid of us," she told her husband. "Even Beany, and she's only eight!"

"Beany is tough," said Mr. Robinson.

"Of course she isn't!"

"Underneath she is!"

"What rubbish! And I always thought the twins enjoyed school, but Ant hasn't stopped telling me how pleased she is to be missing so much of the start of term, and Perry is almost as bad!"

"I used to love the chance of a few days off school," remarked her husband.

"And I couldn't believe Sun Dance! He usually hates any sort of change."

"I don't mind you going at all," Sun Dance had said. "I'd just as soon live with Robin and Mrs. Brogan as here!"

"Oh, Sun Dance!"

"I shouldn't mind at all if you stayed away for years," Sun Dance continued valiantly, and his mother sighed and said she supposed she hadn't been much fun lately.

"No, you jolly well haven't!" agreed Sun Dance. "Robin's mum is far more fun. And her house is a lot warmer, and she's a much better cook—"

"Yes, THANK YOU, Sun Dance," interrupted Mr. Robinson at this point.

"And she's prettier," continued Sun Dance, ignoring him, "and she won't keep me awake at night, coughing and coughing! Ow! Put me down! Where are you taking me?"

"Just out of range," said Mr. Robinson, dumping him in the kitchen. "What *are* you thinking of, Sun Dance? Talking to your mother like that!"

"I thought you said to act pleased," said Sun Dance indignantly. "That's the best acting pleased I can do! I thought it was jolly good! I didn't say any of the things I really think."

"Didn't you?" asked Mr. Robinson, twinkling down at him. "What do you really think?"

"I think, 'What if they never come back? I don't know how long they're going for—'"

"A week," interrupted Mr. Robinson. "I told you a week."

"'Or so,' you said," said Sun Dance. "'Or so.' I heard you."

"A week and a day," said his father. "Eight days. Nothing."

"Eight days!" repeated Sun Dance. "I didn't know it would be *eight days!* Eight days is ages! What if there's sharks in the sea at Barbados and Mum goes swimming? What about our house? It will all be empty, anything might come in—or anyone! And the waves look like great white lions, tearing to get at the house. It will be awful without Perry and Ant. Perry and Ant are the brave ones. I'm not brave . . ."

"Of course you are! And you *did* do brilliantly, acting pleased. You are the bravest of all. I put you in charge!"

"In charge?" asked Sun Dance. "In charge of what?"

"Everything," said Mr. Robinson magnificently. "The family silver, your mum's new vacuum cleaner. The lot!" said Mr. Robinson.

It was a great relief to everyone when they could stop behaving like heroes—when Mr. and Mrs. Robinson had finally driven away and they could sit in Mrs. Brogan's candlelit living room (because the power was off again) and tell each other how noble they had been, and think of all the wishes they would wish on Freya's sword. Not that anyone except Beany really believed in dolphin luck, but it was an easy way of passing the time.

"Mum better," said Ant. "And Old Blanket come back alive."

"No, no," said Perry hastily. "I read a story about someone who wished that once. Not come back alive; in dog heaven. Much safer!"

"All right, Old Blanket definitely safe in heaven," said Ant. "And another dog for us."

"You can share Friday," offered Robin.

"It's not the same," said Ant. "But thanks. What would you ask for?"

"Nothing." Robin would not even pretend to believe in magic. In the year following the death of his father, he had wished a lifetime's empty wishes and then given up forever.

"Perry and Ant not going away," said Beany. "I'd just like that. And everything to be back to normal."

Ant immediately agreed.

"Ordinary school and ordinary home and no Mad Aunt Mabel—"

"Don't start disliking your poor aunt before you even meet her," interrupted Mrs. Brogan. "Your father says she's kindness itself, and he should know. Meanwhile, there's nothing like getting on with the next job when you're down in the dumps. Ant, have you got the tickets?"

"Is it time to go?"

"Just about. Perry, money? And tell me where you get off."

"Hemingford."

"Hemingford *North*. It is just a little branch line; you shouldn't have any trouble. The journey takes about an hour and your aunt will be there to meet you. Now listen! As soon as you arrive safely, I want you to drop this post-card in the post office mailbox, just so we'll know that you've gotten there if the phone lines happen to be down again. And telephone as soon as you can. Promise?"

Perry and Ant nodded.

"Don't forget then. Tickets. Money. Where do you get off?"

"Hemingford North," chanted Perry and Ant dutifully.

"Then what?"

"Postcard to tell you we're there, and telephone as soon as we can."

"Sure you know the number?"

"Of course."

"Write it down in case you forget. Now then, it's time I was getting the car out, so get your bags and be saying good-bye while I bring it round."

"Can't we come with you to see them off?" asked Beany.

"It would be much better if you stayed here with Robin and Friday. Nothing more depressing than freezing good-byes on station platforms. Two minutes, Perry and Ant. We haven't much time."

As it turned out, there was no time at all. The train was almost ready to leave as they reached the station. Perry and Ant just managed to jump aboard and grab the rucksacks Mrs. Brogan hurled after them.

"Hemingford *North!*" she shouted as the whistle blew. "Courage! Courage!"

"We'll be all right," called back Ant. "And thank you very much!"

A furious gust of snow-filled wind slammed against

the train. Perry and Ant lurched back from the window, pawing their eyes, and when they looked again, everything familiar—Mrs. Brogan, the station, the whole outside world—was suddenly gone.

"Well, we've been wanting proper snow for ages," said Perry bravely.

"Yes," said Ant.

"Perhaps she'll have a sled we could borrow."

"Yes."

"Or we could make one."

"Yes."

"Come on, Ant! What about what Mrs. Brogan said? We've got to get on with the next job."

"I am," said Ant, whose most immediate task at that moment was to stop herself from howling with misery.

"I knew you'd be like this."

Ant sniffed.

"So I brought a lot of things to cheer you up." With school and illness and Sun Dance left behind, Perry's natural optimism was already beginning to return.

"I don't need cheering up," said Ant ungratefully.

"Twiglets," continued Perry, digging vigorously in his rucksack. "And bananas! And you remember that time just before Christmas when Old Blanket tried to catch the mailman and his teeth sank into the gate instead . . ."

"You know he was only playing!"

"He was growling really loud!"

"Only pretend growling."

"It was dead weird the way his fur stood up in a line right down his back! And that was a fantastic jump the mailman did over the wall!"

"He was only showing off!"

"He dropped his bag though. I wonder what people thought when they got Christmas cards with bite marks all over them. Anyway, you know how Old Blanket tried to tear down the gate to get at him, and one of his teeth came out and got stuck in the wood . . ."

"Poor darling Old Blanket," said Ant.

"Well, I've got that tooth!" concluded Perry in triumph. "It's in with my toothbrush so it doesn't get lost!"

"Perry! You haven't really! Oh, let me see it!"

"And I've brought loads of other things too. That book you like about the man-eating tigers"—Perry pulled out a tattered paperback—"stacks of nuts, and the nutcrackers! And your old Panda!"

"Have you brought Panda?" exclaimed Ant. "I looked everywhere for Panda to bring, and I couldn't find him anywhere."

"I'd probably already packed him," said Perry smugly.

At Porridge Hall Mrs. Brogan huddled by the fire and shook and shook with cold.

"That station was absolutely arctic!" she exclaimed. "Oh well, at least we've got the electricity back! When did it come on?"

"Just after you left," Robin told her. "And the telephone is working again as well. There was a call from Sun Dance and Beany's school . . ."

"They didn't mind them not being there today? Mr. Robinson said he'd written to explain."

"They're closed!" Sun Dance told her.

"What!"

"That's why they telephoned. They're calling everyone to say they're closed. They can't get the heating working. Something's burst and all the downstairs classrooms are flooded!"

"Good grief!"

"And Dan's mum rang as well," Robin told her. "To ask if I'd like to go and stay with them until the weather gets better. To save me biking back and forth to school every day."

"I don't mind driving you in to school while the weather is so dreadful. I was going to take you all."

"And just before you came in Mad Aunt Mabel called to see if Perry and Ant had gotten off all right. I said I thought so, but I wasn't sure because you weren't back from the station. She said she'd call back."

"Oh good."

"She sounded nice."

"Of course, she's nice!"

"And we put the television on, and the weather forecast said gales reaching storm force along the east coast!"

Perry and Ant, traveling steadily inland, noticed that the wind was nothing like so wild as it had been at home.

"But just look at the snow!" said Perry. "We never have snow like this at home!"

Mile after mile of snow-covered countryside was flashing past the windows. In the whole white landscape, there seemed to be no movement at all. The heat of the train and the stillness outside made them very drowsy. They sat half asleep with the contents of Perry's rucksack strewn about them.

"We're slowing down!" said Ant suddenly. "Quick, Perry! We must be nearly there! This might be the station!"

Perry leaped to his feet and began grabbing his possessions and bundling them together. Ant groveled on the floor to collect scattered nuts.

"Come and help me squash everything back in!" begged Perry. "Push it down as hard as you can while I try and fasten a strap!"

"Have you got Old Blanket's tooth?"

"I don't know. I must have. Panda! There's Panda left out! You were sitting on him! Look, we've just passed a sign; it *is* the station!"

"Check you've got Old Blanket's tooth!"

Perry plunged an arm deep into his rucksack, found his sponge bag, and yanked it up.

"Yes, I did put it back. I knew I had. Fancy you nearly leaving Panda! Oh, we've stopped! Quick!"

With not a moment to spare they yanked open the door, threw out their rucksacks, and tumbled down onto the platform.

CASTLE HEMINGFORD, read a huge white sign above their heads.

There was a doorless waiting room, a boarded-up ticket office, and that was all.

"She's not here," said Ant.

"What? What?" asked Perry distractedly as he stood gazing up at the station sign. "What did you say?"

"There's nobody here. No Mad Aunt Mabel. No one at all . . . Oh Perry!"

All at once Ant understood the reason for her brother's mesmerized expression.

"Castle Hemingford!" she wailed.

"Yes," said Perry. "It's not her who's not here. It's us that's not there."

After awhile they pulled themselves together and began to look around.

"Castle Hemingford," read Perry from a glass-covered timetable they discovered on a wall. "Hemingford. Hemingford North. It's my fault. I just saw it said Hemingford as we flashed past. I should have looked properly. There's not another train for two more hours!"

"Well at least there's a train sometime," said Ant, suddenly determined to be cheerful. "Courage, courage, that's what Mrs. Brogan said. What do you think we ought to do?"

"Telephone Porridge Hall and tell them what's happened," said Perry at once. "And then see what else is here."

It did not take long to do that. Castle Hemingford consisted of nothing at all—no telephone, no shops, and no houses.

"Not even a castle," said Ant. "Unless it's somewhere down the road."

Neither of them felt much like going off to explore, and the waiting room was far too cold to spend any amount of time in, so they passed what was left of the two hours in building a snowman outside the ticket-office door.

"It's years since we had enough snow to do anything with," remarked Perry, watching critically while Ant balanced extra snow on the snowman's head. "What's that supposed to be?"

"A motorbike helmet. I'm turning him into a snow Aunt Mabel. Do you think she'll meet the next train?"

"Bound to." Perry gave the snow Aunt Mabel a huge hooked nose and black gravel eyes. "Bound to; but I don't suppose she'll be very pleased."

"This one doesn't look very pleased either," said Ant.

That was true. The snow Aunt Mabel was beginning to look quite sinister, not at all the sort of company anyone would chose to have around on such a desolate afternoon. They gave her dead-grass hair and stick fingers, and then, feeling distinctly uneasy, a yellow banana smile.

"Crikey," said Perry, standing back to get the full effect of the smile. "I hope she's not really like that!"

It was quite a relief to hear the rumble of the train arriving, to jump aboard and wave good-bye to their horrible creation.

"If the weather warms up, she'll have melted before we come back," said Ant thankfully.

This time they did not even bother to go and look for seats on the train. They waited anxiously at the door, peering out into the gray afternoon. An empty platform slid into view and disappeared, but the train did not stop.

"That must have been Hemingford," said Perry. "Only a minute or two to go now. Get ready!"

They were out almost before the train had stopped.

"Oy! You two!" bawled an angry voice down the line.

"Us?" asked Ant.

"You two!"

It was the guard, glaring furiously from an open win-

dow of the train. "Just you be a bit more careful in the future!"

"What?"

"Let the train stop another time! Daft silly thing to do
that was! Might have been an accident!"

"Horrible old man," muttered Perry. He spoke just at
the moment of clear silence between the blowing of the
whistle and the departure of the train.

"I heard that!" shouted the guard, and pulled up the
window.

"Don't care if you did," muttered Perry untruthfully,
and, to show how much he did not care, waved defiantly
at the departing train. "And don't you start blubbering
again!" he added to Ant.

This was so unfair that it was with a slight feeling of
triumph that Ant silently pointed at the snowy notice
looming above them.

HEMINGFORD

"We've done it again," said Ant.

Hemingford Station was identical in every way to its
predecessor, but this time they did not build a snowman.
They sat hunched in the waiting room, which had a door,
and waited for the next train.

"Nothing must go wrong with this one," said Perry.
"Because there isn't another."

four
•••••••

"Dad's put me in charge," Sun Dance had told Perry as he watched him pack.

"Excellent," said Perry warmly. "Fantastic. Nothing to worry about then."

"There might easily be burglars."

"Oh, I don't suppose so. Dad wouldn't want you to worry about burglars."

"I *shouldn't* worry!"

"Good."

"I could soon take care of burglars. Easy. No problem."

"How?" asked Perry, bored but patient.

"Trap 'em."

"Kids can't trap burglars," said Perry, laughing and hating himself for laughing. "I tell you what, I nearly forgot; I must remember to pack my snake. Hey! Are you crying?"

"No, I'm NOT!" said Sun Dance.

*　*　*

"Sun Dance," said Mrs. Brogan. "What *are* you doing?"

"Listening," replied Sun Dance, peering out at her from the cupboard under the stairs. "I can hear bumps and a sort of ticking. Come and see if you can too."

"I can't just now. Perry and Ant might phone any minute, and I don't want to miss them."

"They won't," said Sun Dance. "The phone's stopped working again."

"Oh no!"

"The wire that's fixed to the house has come off. Robin found it just now when he went out with Friday. It had blown right across the grass. He's rolled it up so it's out of the way. He said to tell you."

"Well, why *didn't* you tell me?" demanded Mrs. Brogan.

"I am," Sun Dance replied patiently. "I'm telling you now. And about the bumps and the ticking."

"Grrrr!" growled Mrs. Brogan, half annoyed and half amused at such casualness, but all the same she got down on her hands and knees and crawled into the cupboard. There Sun Dance was crouched with his head pressed to the wall that divided Porridge Hall into two houses.

"Listen!" ordered Sun Dance, so Mrs. Brogan obligingly listened, and after a few seconds she said that the bumps were caused by the central heating, and the ticking was the electricity meter whirling around above Sun Dance's head.

"And that reminds me," she added, "the washing

machine must have nearly finished, and I must get it loaded up again before we have another power cut."

"Is that really all you think the noises are?" asked Sun Dance. "Electricity and the heating?" and he looked so disappointed that Mrs. Brogan was sorry for him. She had heard that he had been put in charge and understood that it was hard to be in charge of nothing.

"We'll go on a burglar hunt as soon as I've finished in the kitchen," she promised.

Ten minutes later they were both in the Robinson half of Porridge Hall inspecting the empty rooms. Despite the fact that the heating had been left on and everything was where it had always been, the house without its occupants felt so terribly dismal that Mrs. Brogan watched rather anxiously as Sun Dance prowled the rooms.

"It's very strange," he said.

"What is?"

"There being no one here."

Mrs. Brogan, who was very fond of Sun Dance, reached down and hugged him and said before he knew it everyone would be back again and it would be as if they'd never been away.

"I didn't mean any of us," explained Sun Dance, wriggling out of the hug to peer into the bathroom linen cupboard. "I meant anyone else."

"Oh, Sun Dance!"

"Haven't we got anything anyone wants?"

Mrs. Brogan thoughtlessly remarked that she was sure they had hundreds of things dozens of people would want, and Sun Dance looked very pleased and said that was exactly what he thought himself.

Mrs. Brogan groaned.

"We'll just have to keep a really close watch," said Sun Dance with satisfaction.

"Well, I'm going home to do some baking with Beany," said Mrs. Brogan, realizing she had worried quite unnecessarily about Sun Dance's feelings. "Are you coming with me, or do you want to stay a bit longer?"

"Stay a bit longer, please," replied Sun Dance, whose head was already fizzing with plans.

As soon as Mrs. Brogan had gone, he set about getting together the materials for the Standard Robinson Person Trap, perfected years earlier by its inventor, Perry Robinson, and passed on by practical demonstration to his brother and sisters (whom it never failed to surprise). It consisted of a baking tray balanced on the top of a half-open door and loaded with a variety of articles, according to what was available and for whom it was intended. (Perry's greatest success had been a huge pile of snow and his least popular, a large dead jellyfish.)

Sun Dance's trap, designed with the dual intention of terrifying its victim and alerting its inventor, was constructed so as to produce the maximum amount of noise. On top of his baking tray above the hall door, he positioned Old Blanket's enamel water bowl, Beany's xylophone, and the string of cowbells that Mad Aunt Mabel had sent from Switzerland.

"It works but it's not half loud enough," he decided after testing Trap Mark 1 by the simple method of pushing open the door and catching himself.

Burglar Trap Mark 2 was much more ambitious. He swapped the baking tray for the enormous roasting pan in which the Christmas turkeys had been cremated, and in it he arranged a large container of black pepper, a can full of marbles, and an open bottle of permanent black ink.

"So even if he runs away, we'll know which one he is," Sun Dance told himself.

"Unless he's got black hair," he added after a few moments of further thought.

In case he had black hair, Sun Dance added a pot of red poster paint and carefully spread newspapers on the carpet beneath to avoid any unnecessary mess.

"There!" he said with satisfaction, and wished that someone was on hand to admire it. For a moment he thought of fetching Beany and Mrs. Brogan and then discarded the idea. In the old days Perry would have been the one to really appreciate the burglar trap, but Perry was endless frozen miles away.

"But not now," thought Sun Dance. "He thinks I'm a kid. And he packed my snake to make me think he liked it. I shall catch a real burglar! That would show him! Then he couldn't say I wasn't Sun Dance anymore!"

Suddenly the house felt very lonely and the thought of Mrs. Brogan and Beany baking in the kitchen was rather comforting.

"Should I test it?" he asked himself, taking one last look at his invention before he left, "or not?"

"Not," said Sun Dance to Sun Dance, and he tiptoed out of the house.

HEMINGFORD NORTH, read the sign.

"Hemingford North!" said Perry, absolutely triumphant, as he bounced onto the platform. "Hemingford North! Can you see a mailbox?"

"What for?"

"Mrs. Brogan's postcard to tell her everything is all right. Yes, good, there's one in that wall!"

"But everything isn't all right," protested Ant, hurrying after him. "Everything's wrong! We're four hours late, and there's no one to meet us . . . Perry!"

"What?"

"You shouldn't have mailed it!"

"We're here, aren't we?" demanded Perry.

"Yes, but . . ."

"Well then. Hey, Ant! Sniff!"

"What? Where are you going now?"

Perry, snuffling the frosty air, was heading toward the exit.

"Can't you smell it?" he asked.

"Smell what?"

"Chips! Hurry up! There must be a chip shop close by!"

"But we can't just go off and buy chips!" exclaimed Ant.

"Why not?"

Ant could think of lots of reasons why not. "Mad Aunt Mabel might arrive at the station looking for us while we are away. Mad Aunt Mabel (should she arrive) will have cooked us supper and won't be pleased if we are full of chips and can't eat it. It will be black dark soon and Mad Aunt Mabel might not arrive at all. Mad Aunt Mabel might easily have given up hope of us altogether, in which case a state of extreme panic is the immediate priority. And how mad," asked Ant, "might Mad Aunt Mabel actually be? Or don't you care?"

Perry, who had suddenly discovered himself to be starving to death, listened impatiently to all this and then pointed out that since they were four hours late, any supper prepared for them would undoubtedly be ruined, that at any rate he personally had space enough inside for any number of suppers, that it never got really black dark when it was snowy, that Ant could wait for Mad Aunt Mabel if she liked while he went chip shopping, and finally that if no one should arrive to meet them, the thing to do would be to telephone Porridge Hall and explain the situation to Mrs. Brogan.

"We'll do that now!" said Ant, heading for the station telephone booth. "I don't know why I didn't think of it before."

"You're just in a flap because you're hungry," said Perry cheerfully, but even he went rather quiet when they dialed Porridge Hall and discovered that once again the telephone lines were down.

"Now what?" asked Ant.

"Wait here while I get those chips, and then we'll think of something."

"We don't even know where she lives."

"Somebody will. I'll ask at the chip shop."

"We don't even know her *name!*"

"So we don't!" said Perry after a moment's startled thought. "Oh well."

"What's the good of saying 'Oh well'?"

"What's the good of wailing?" asked Perry. "Mrs. Brogan would say that the thing to do is get on with the next job, and the next job is something to eat. And this place isn't any size at all. She can't be far away!"

That was true. As far as they could make out, Hemingford North was nothing more than a station, a short dark street, and the chip shop. Perry headed at once for the chip shop and returned a few minutes later hugging a large fragrant parcel and looking relieved and apprehensive at the same time.

"I've found where she lives anyway," he announced. "The boy who was buying chips ahead of me knew."

"You're looking for *what?*" the boy had asked. He was a lot bigger than Perry and at least two years older, with an intimidating swagger about him.

"Our aunt Mabel," said Perry, feeling an utter fool.

"Your aunt Mabel?"

"Mad Aunt Mabel we call her," said Perry, regretting every word as he spoke. "She lives round here."

"Mad, did you say?"

"Well, maddish," said Perry modestly.

"Not her up on the hill?"

"I don't know. She might be up on the hill. We're supposed to be going to stay with her but she hasn't come to meet the train."

"I wouldn't fancy stopping up there," said the boy.

"Do you know her, then?"

"I know who you mean," said his informer, and sniggered.

"She's our godmother."

"Godmother!"

"And related. Great-aunt. She's been going round the world on a motorbike."

"It must run in the family!" said the boy.

"What must?" asked Perry before he could stop himself.

"Oh, nothing. No offense. You going up there tonight, then?"

"I suppose so," said Perry doubtfully. "Could you show me where she lives?"

"Certainly," agreed the boy with mock politeness, and had waited until they were both served and then stepped into the street and pointed far up the snowy hillside.

"Where that light is," he told Perry.

"Crikey!" said Perry.

Sun Dance's burglar trap caught Mrs. Brogan when late at night she braved the terrible weather to check that all was well next door. Fortunately the poster paint and black ink just missed landing on top of her, but nothing else did. The can of marbles caught her fair and square on the back of her head while the pepper billowed in an enormous cloud around her.

"Oh! Oh! Oh!" gasped Mrs. Brogan gulping in deep lungfuls of it as she fell over the xylophone. "Whatever . . . !" (She sneezed seven times very quickly.) "Whatever . . . ! Whatever . . . ! *What* am I standing in?"

"Paint," said Sun Dance, materializing in pajamas in front of her.

"Sun Dance!" exclaimed Mrs. Brogan, and sneezed and sneezed.

"Good thing I put the paper down," said Sun Dance

virtuously. "It was a burglar trap I made. What do you think?"

Mrs. Brogan, speechless, glared at him from streaming eyes.

"Fantastic, eh?" said Sun Dance proudly.

Nothing Perry had eaten before—no carefully cooked Sunday dinner, no birthday party food, no private bedroom feast with friends—had ever tasted as good as the half-warm, half-tough, half-soggy, wholly delicious fish and chips he and Ant consumed together on the long road up to the house on the hill. It was a very long road indeed, single track, running between high stone walls. Deep snow was piled on either side.

"They must have had a snowplow up here," remarked Perry between mouthfuls.

"What?" asked Ant, still horribly preoccupied by the unanswered question of how mad Mad Aunt Mabel would actually be.

"A snowplow."

"Oh, yes."

"Are you all right?"

"Yes, yes."

"Brilliant chips!"

"Yes," agreed Ant, chewing valiantly.

"Soon be there."

The last thing Ant wanted was to soon be there. She would have preferred the frozen trek to last all night rather than reach the end of it. Not even Perry's persistent cheerfulness could dispel her certainty that the worst was yet to come.

"Are you cold?" asked Perry.

"Not really." Ant hugged the extra portion of fish and chips, bought as a peace offering to their hostess and now wedged between her sweater and jacket, and continued her plodding.

"I wonder if we'll remember her when we see her. We were only four. Can you remember that far back?" asked Perry.

"No."

"I can just remember Beany being born. We were four then."

Ant said nothing.

"And the birthday when Sun Dance ate Mum's little gold watch because he wanted to tick."

"That was when we were six."

"It was the same summer that we went to choose Old Blanket at the RSPCA kennels. We were going to choose the one with the saddest face. Only they were all sad. So we chose the biggest, and Dad was angry."

Ant sniffed.

"But I can't ever remember meeting Mad Aunt Mabel."

Ant continued her silent trudging.

"Oh, well," said Perry.

Halfway through their journey the road turned at right angles to cut around the top of the hill, and the way became a stony, rutted cart track. Only a narrow path through the snow was clear enough for them to walk along in single file.

"Tomorrow we'll dig her out properly," Perry announced as he led the way. "No wonder she couldn't keep meeting the trains."

"Perry!" called Ant from far behind. "Perry! Perry! Stop for a minute!"

"We're nearly there," said Perry.

"I know," said Ant.

The door was black. Blistered, peeling black paint, with an old-fashioned latch, an enormous keyhole, and a massive iron knocker.

"It's only a matter of getting on with the next job," said Perry, and knocked.

At once, almost beneath his hand, the door swung open. There was an enormous flood of noise, a torrent of barking mingled with harsh screams, and a yowling swirl of movement at his feet.

"Look at that now!" exclaimed a tiny, silvery voice. "The cats are out!"

Perry and Ant, too surprised to reply, stared and stared.

She's not much bigger than Beany, was Perry's first impression, while Ant struggled to collect any thoughts at all. Whatever she had expected, it had not been this. No one so old, no one so unearthly, no one so like a handful of brown leaves, bright rags, thistledown, and feathers, brushed up into a corner and molded into life.

"The cats are out," repeated this utter stranger at the door, "but they'll be back, and I have two big dogs here yet. So what do you think of that?"

Was that a threat, Ant wondered, *the mention of the two big dogs?* Were they meant to be frightened? Astonishment and alarm were jangling and quivering in the air between them. Was she the only one to notice?

"We brought you some chips," said Perry.

"Chips?" repeated the little voice, and almost singing, "Chips and chips and chips and chips—"

"And fish," interrupted Perry, in exactly the voice he used at home when he considered Sun Dance was going too far.

"We're sorry we've been so long coming," put in Ant hastily.

"We got them from the shop down in the village before we came," Perry explained. "In case you hadn't cooked."

"A boy told Perry where you lived, or we'd never have found you," said Ant. "We didn't even know your name. Only Aunt Mabel. Or would you rather we said Great-Aunt?"

They might never have said a word for all the notice that was taken of them.

"Chips and fish and chips and fish," sang the little voice. "Half a pound of treacle! That's the way the money goes! The parrot calls me Tilly!"

"What?"

"Though he worn't always my parrot."

"Worn't he?" repeated Ant, still half mesmerized.

"'Darlin' Tilly,' he tells me. 'Darlin' Tilly. Shut the door and give us a kiss!' So I've come round to the name. That's him screaming still! I told the dogs, but you can't tell a parrot. I have to abide by his wishes."

"Do you?"

"Abide by his wishes. Should you like to see him?"

Without waiting for a reply, she turned and led them

into a little low room, and it was like stepping back in time.

Candlelight and firelight. Bare walls, bare wooden furniture, and a bare stone-flagged floor. Ant had the uncomfortable feeling that they had intruded into a place where they had no right to be, and she was not the only one.

"Tilly!" screeched a parrot in terrible alarm. "Tilly! Tilly! Tilly! Tilly my darlin', you *must* abide by my wishes!"

There was a commotion of scarlet and blue and gold as he flew shrieking and clattering over their heads.

"His name is Samson," said the silver voice from the doorway."Tell him who you are and he'll be still."

"Tell him our names?" asked Ant.

"And he'll be still," said the parrot's owner.

"Tilly, this is too much!" screamed the parrot. "Too much! Too much! Too much! Too much . . ."

"Perry!" bawled Perry, above the din. "Our names are Perry and Ant! Perry and Ant!"

It made no difference. The noise, if anything, grew louder, and the room seemed full of brilliant, beating feathers.

"Peregrine and Antoinette," shouted Ant suddenly. "Peregrine and Antoinette!"

"Tilly my darlin'," said the parrot faintly, and was still.

"But nobody calls us that!" protested Perry.

"Peregrine and Antoinette," said their hostess from the doorway. "And Tilly and Samson. Those are the names he has given us, and we *must* abide by his wishes. The cats are called nothing at all."

"Nothing at all?"

"He won't allow it."

"What about the dogs?" asked Ant, gazing toward the two black-and-white collies that had appeared in the doorway.

"Mary and Joseph."

"Mary and Joseph!"

"Christmas Eve, they arrived. Worn out."

Suddenly Ant found that she was crying. Huge tears poured down her cheeks and her nose began to run. She groped desperately inside her jacket for something to wipe it on and dropped the packet of chips.

"Tilly my love," moaned the parrot in despair as Perry picked them up.

"Ant," hissed Perry, and then, at a filthy look from the parrot, "Antoinette! Stop it! Don't! What will she think?"

But Ant was past caring what anyone thought. Old Blanket's death, her mother's illness, the journey and coldness and confusion now overwhelmed her completely.

"Oh, *please* stop it!" begged Perry in agony. "Aunt Mab . . . I mean Tilly . . . can we put our bags and things somewhere? She's only tired. She'll be fine in the morning."

There was no answer. He turned to the doorway, and there was nobody there.

"She's gone," said Ant, between sodden gulps. "Oh, I wish I could go to bed!"

"I expect you can," replied Perry as comfortingly as he could. "I'll go and ask her."

She was in the snowy garden, singing into the dark.

"Aunt Ma . . ." began Perry, shivering in the night wind that had begun to sweep the dark hillside.

"I'm Tilly," she interrupted. "Tilly, Tilly. The cats are on their way."

"Good," said Perry, not caring at all. "Good. But about Ant. Can she go to bed, do you think? Where are we going to sleep, please?"

"To sleep?" asked Tilly, after a few moments of utter silence.

"Yes."

"Perchance to dream?"

"Er . . . Yes, I suppose."

"The cats sleep in boxes. Four boxes. Four cats, four boxes. Trained to it."

"But what about us?"

"Not in boxes," mused Tilly, thinking aloud. "Too big, you are. Nor trained to it."

Perry waited patiently.

"Not in my bed," continued Tilly firmly. "That would be too much! Not in the henhouse of course, nor out in a shed, nor under a hedge . . ."

Perry glanced behind him and hoped very much that Ant was not listening to these remarks.

"It will have to be Mary and Joseph's bed!" announced Tilly triumphantly. "The very thing!"

"What, both of us?" exclaimed Perry.

"And Mary and Joseph," said Tilly happily.

Mary and Joseph, it turned out, slept upstairs on their own large double bed. There was plenty of room in it for Perry and Ant to sleep; there were even clean sheets (provided at Perry's request by a slightly astonished Tilly). Mary and Joseph did not appear to mind at all, and nobody who had slept with Old Blanket in his declining years could have possibly objected to the arrangement.

"She's terribly strange," said Ant wearily, as they settled down for the night.

"Well, we knew that before we came."

"I'm glad Mary and Joseph are here. They're nice. It's a bit like having Old Blanket back."

"Except they don't smell," Perry tactlessly agreed.

Ant, who was nearly asleep, dragged herself awake enough to answer, "I *liked* the way Old Blanket smelled!" and Perry, realizing she was getting better, smiled into the darkness.

"They probably don't snore either," he added, but this time there was no reply.

five
......

On Tuesday morning the card that Perry had so rashly posted on the platform at Hemingford North arrived at Porridge Hall.

"Arrived safely. Perry and Ant Robinson," it read in Mrs. Brogan's own handwriting.

Mrs. Brogan received it from the mailman with a sigh of relief.

"That's one thing less to worry about, then," she remarked.

"Looking a bit under the weather, you are this morning," the mailman commented. "Under the weather, eh?" and he roared with laughter at his own joke. "Terrible though, isn't it? We've had nothing like it for years."

"It's not very nice," admitted Mrs. Brogan.

"And they've said it is getting worse!"

"Surely not," said Mrs. Brogan, mopping her streaming eyes and thinking crossly that the mailman was secretly enjoying his bad news.

"Hoping your roof will last it out, I dare say? Shocking cold you've got!"

"Nothing," Mrs. Brogan assured him sniffily, determined not to give him another misfortune to gloat over. "Nothing, nothing. A touch of chill!"

"Brandy and warm milk!" ordered the mailman bossily.

"I can't bear warm milk."

"With a raw egg in it. Coats the throat!"

Mrs. Brogan involuntarily covered her ears.

"Lost that dog of theirs next door, haven't they?" he continued cheerfully.

"Yes, I'm afraid so," said Mrs. Brogan.

"Worst animal on the route! Well, I must be getting on. Looking very nasty, indeed you are, if you ask me!"

"Well, I didn't!" muttered Mrs. Brogan crossly, although when she looked into the hall mirror after he had gone, she was forced to admit he was right.

"Very nasty!" she said aloud. The effects of Sun Dance's burglar trap had lasted all night, and she was still sneezing as vigorously as ever. Sun Dance himself was completely overwhelmed by the success of his achievement and alternated between feelings of awful remorse and secret, dazzled pride.

"When Perry telephones, will you tell him?" he asked Mrs. Brogan hopefully. "Perry made one with a dead jellyfish once."

"Well, thank goodness you didn't have one of those on hand," said Mrs. Brogan.

"It wouldn't have been any good if I had. I needed noise. A dead jellyfish would have been much too quiet."

"Much too dead as well," said Robin. "Poor old Mum!

Pepper was bad enough. Lucky for you it was only her you caught! A real burglar would have been furious."

"I am slightly furious myself," admitted Mrs. Brogan. "It wasn't just the pepper; there was half a ton of hardware in that roasting pan! What if I'd been knocked out?"

"No burglarizing," said Sun Dance with satisfaction.

Mrs. Brogan glared at him across the breakfast table and tenderly mopped her nose.

"What you made was a burglar annoyer," Beany told Sun Dance. "Not a burglar trap. It wouldn't have trapped anyone, and now Mrs. Brogan is ill."

"I think we should forget the subject," said Mrs. Brogan, seeing that Sun Dance was beginning to sniff rather ominously. "Of course I'm not ill; anyone would have a headache after being landed on by that enormous can of marbles! It will be completely better by lunchtime, you wait and see!"

"All the same," said Robin, "perhaps I will stay at Dan's after school tonight. It would save you having to come and fetch me if the mailman is right and the weather really does get worse."

"I suppose it would."

"You *don't* look very well!"

"I'm quite all right, but if you really don't mind, it would be a great help. Perhaps you'd better get a few things together."

"I already have," said Robin.

That afternoon Porridge Hall was quieter than Sun Dance or Beany had ever imagined possible. Friday, who knew quite well that Robin would not be back that night, was curled in a tight and reproachful ball on his master's bed and declining all offers of comfort. The telephone was still out of action, the television aerial had blown down, and Mrs. Brogan had refused to give Sun Dance the key to the other half of Porridge Hall.

"Well, there must be another way through," said Sun Dance. "There must be doors in the walls from when it was all one big house."

"Blocked off years ago," Mrs. Brogan told him.

"What about the cellar?" asked Sun Dance.

"It was divided when the central heating was put in."

"The attic then?"

"The attic stairs were taken down when I was about fourteen or so. They were woodwormy and my parents were afraid of it spreading into the roof. Nobody ever used the attic anyway; it didn't have a proper floor so the stairs were never replaced. Give up, Sun Dance!"

Sun Dance did not give up. He spent the next hour searching for secret panels. He stuck his head up the dining-room chimney and wondered if it could possibly be connected with the chimneys next door. He inspected all the bedroom closets in case one of them should happen to have a magic back. He invented a new burglar trap and set it up to catch Beany in order to test that it really worked. Then he went and lay on his bed and gazed at the trapdoor over his head and waited to see what would happen.

Mrs. Brogan, dozing on the sofa and trying not to think of how ill she felt, gave a small scream as something cold and soggy was placed on her hot, tired eyes.

"Teabags," Beany told her. "Gran used to do it."

"Gran?" asked Mrs. Brogan.

"Dead Gran," explained Beany unsentimentally. "She did lots of things like that, but Dad always said they were rubbish and antibiotics were the thing."

"That does sound like your father," agreed Mrs. Brogan, laughing.

"Do your eyes feel any better?"

"Much better," said Mrs. Brogan. "Thank you, Beany."

"I've got some medicine cooking for you in the kitchen."

"I hope you haven't been touching the stove!"

"I only put a little saucepan on the hot plate. Black currant jam and water and lemon juice. I've got a little book of recipes that used to be Gran's."

"It sounds very nice, but you'd better let me lift the saucepan off again."

"It's a homemade book, full of written-out cures for things. Dad wouldn't let me try them on Mum. Mrs. Brogan, do you feel too poorly to talk?"

"Of course I don't!" exclaimed Mrs. Brogan, sitting up at once. "What do you want to talk about, Beany?"

"What happened to Freya's magic sword? You said it was found. Found and then lost again."

"I think that's probably as far as the story goes."

Beany thought that this could not possibly be correct, and after a long investigation in the recipe book, she added another ingredient to Mrs. Brogan's black currant tea.

* * *

Sun Dance's second burglar trap worked just as well as his first had done. A trail of the unsuspecting victim's own possessions lured her up to her bedroom, where she was catapulted through the door by means of a carefully placed trip wire and locked in before she had time to begin her first indignant howl.

Nobody could have been sorrier than Sun Dance was when he saw the size of the bump on his sister's head. He crawled into the cupboard under the stairs and refused to come out.

"Poor old Beany!" said Mrs. Brogan, when she had finished telling Sun Dance what she thought of him, picked up the victim, and dismantled the trap. "Poor old Beany! What can I do to cheer you up?"

"Nothing," said Beany dolefully.

"Let's find you something cold to put on that bump anyway. Come into the kitchen and I'll get you some ice. That's another old-fashioned remedy!"

"You didn't drink your black currant tea."

"I was just going to fetch it when I heard you fall. I shall try it straightaway . . . Oh!"

"What?"

"Beany, has it got sticks in it?"

"Only little bits."

"Little bits of what? I think I ought to know before I drink it."

"Rosemary," said Beany, valiantly rubbing her bump with ice cubes. "It will clear your brain and help your memory. It says so in my book. Then you'll be able to tell me what happened to Freya's dolphin sword."

"Will I?"

"Couldn't you try? Some dolphin luck would be very useful."

"I'll do my best," said Mrs. Brogan as she strained the tea. "Rosemary for remembrance! I think that's Shakespeare I'm quoting! This smells quite nice."

Beany watched anxiously while she sipped, and something, perhaps the rosemary tea or perhaps the hopeful expression in Beany's eyes, caused Mrs. Brogan to remember a little bit more.

"It must have been before my grandfather's time that the sword was rediscovered because it was he who used to tell me the story. Perhaps it was his mother who actually found it."

"Someone from Porridge Hall?" asked Beany, astounded.

"Didn't I tell you that? Yes, someone from Porridge Hall. One of the girls."

"Wasn't she grown up?"

"Oh, no! No, I'm sure she wasn't, or it wouldn't have disappeared again, would it? It would have been sold or sent to a museum. Something sensible and boring like that."

"If I found it," interrupted Beany eagerly. "I wouldn't sell it, not for anything. I'd keep it to wish on."

"Of course you would. You'd have to keep it somewhere safe though, and only use it now and then, or people would begin to suspect."

"I could just use it for emergency wishes."

"So you could."

"How old do you think the girl was who found it?"

"Quite little, I imagine. Perhaps about Freya's age when she lost it. Eightish or nineish."

"That's not little!"

"Isn't it?"

"I am eight and a half," pointed out Beany, "and I'm not little! Could it really, honestly grant wishes?"

"In the story it could," said Mrs. Brogan cautiously.

"Is there really such a thing as dolphin luck?"

"In the story there was," said Mrs. Brogan.

That same Tuesday morning Ant awoke early, long before Perry.

While the gray snowy light of the winter morning grew gradually brighter, she lay in bed and thought about the events of the last twenty-four hours.

"This time yesterday I was in bed at home," she told herself, and she closed her eyes and tried to imagine she was still there, and it was like trying to conjure up the landscape of a dream. Too much had happened in between. Her parents had driven away wrapped in scarves and raincoats with suitcases full of summer clothes. Later Mrs. Brogan had driven Perry and herself through gales and snow to catch the train; and then the unbelievable journey inland had followed. After that everything became rather muddled in Ant's mind. A chip shop and a snowy road, with Mad Aunt Mabel at the end of it.

"Tilly," thought Ant, and as if in confirmation she heard a faint voice from the room below remark that Tilly, his love, must abide by his wishes. Samson the parrot was awake. Soon the day must be faced. It was no use trying any longer to pretend that this was home.

A long time ago, thought Ant, *when I was much younger, I lived at Porridge Hall.*

Perry woke up all at once and knew immediately where he was and what ought to happen next.

"Breakfast," he said cheerfully, rolling out of bed and tipping Joseph and Mary onto the floor.

Ant thought it extremely unlikely that anything so normal as breakfast could appear on such an abnormal morning, but she kept her thoughts to herself and presently found that she was wrong. There was breakfast in abundance, enormous bowls of porridge and canned milk, cooked by Tilly and served with complete impartiality to dogs and humans alike.

"I love porridge," remarked Perry, scraping his bowl.

"Nothing better," agreed Tilly, "for comfort *or* convenience."

"Much better than cereal," said Perry.

"'Better than stars or water,'" said Tilly, "'Better than voices of winds that sing, Better than any man's fair daughter . . .'"

"What, porridge?" asked Perry, extremely startled.

Ant saw that Tilly was far away in her own thoughts, no longer interested in discussing the merits of porridge for breakfast.

"What, *porridge?*" repeated Perry.

"Hush!" Tilly said severely to Perry. "Hush, I stole them out of the moon!"

"Tilly my love!" exclaimed the parrot.

It was all rather unnerving.

After breakfast Perry and Ant spent the morning clearing paths. They cleared paths because the day before that was what Perry had said they would do. It seemed to

Perry to be very important that one thing, at least, should go as planned, and it was quite good fun shoveling snow with Mary and Joseph for company and the comfortable sounds of ordinary life that floated up to them from the valley below.

"What shall we do when we're finished?" asked Ant.

"Lunch," said Perry. "My breakfast wore off ages ago. I hope it's something filling."

Lunch was very filling. It was porridge again, and Tilly could not conceal her surprise that they should expect anything at all.

"You're good eaters," she commented. "Not that I mind," and she beamed so kindly at Perry that he found himself beaming back. "I like to watch a creature feed," she continued as she ladled him out a second bowlful. "Peregrine and Antoinette! Far better than I expected!"

This was the first time that she had given any indication that she had expected them at all, and it gave Ant the courage to ask, "What did you expect?"

"The worst," said Tilly solemnly. "I didn't know what to think when I saw you coming up my track."

"Oh . . ."

"But the animals took to you at once—"

"Tilly my love," interrupted Samson reprovingly, "this is too much!"

"Not that I can speak for the parrot," said Tilly hastily. "There is nothing to do here but abide by his wishes! Still, the cats were satisfied and the dogs never said a word and so I took heart."

Perry and Ant gazed at her in silence, appalled to discover how much alarm their arrival had caused.

"And now I think it is just as it was meant to be," said Tilly happily.

"Meant to be?"

"The animals have been a worry," continued Tilly. "But nobody wanted them, so how could I leave them? And yet I believe in traveling light."

"I suppose," said Ant, groping to make some sense of the conversation, "you got used to not having much, going round the world for all that time."

"And the less you have," said Perry, "the less there is to leave behind," and he glanced around the room where they were sitting, which was so noticeably furnished with as little as possible. Tilly nodded in agreement and, avoiding the parrot's gaze, whispered conspiratorially, "There will be practically nothing to pack!"

"But are you thinking of going away again?" demanded Perry in astonishment.

"Not a word!" hissed Tilly, "Fur and feathers make her sneeze! Especially feathers!" and she smiled brightly at Samson and remarked in a loud, clear voice, "I must abide by his wishes!"

Samson glowered at her suspiciously before turning his back and beginning to rearrange his feathers.

"Do you think he understands what you're saying?" asked Ant curiously.

"Every word," replied Tilly, and sighed. "Every word! A great burden. Never mind though," she added, brightening up. "Bear ye one another's burdens! I am sure you will manage!"

Perry and Ant, although far from sure exactly what they were expected to manage, eagerly offered to do anything they could. "We always help at home," Ant told Tilly, "so if you need any shopping or anything . . ."

"Shopping?" repeated Tilly.

Perry, glancing at the second lot of empty porridge plates of the day, resolutely took the plunge.

"We wondered if you needed any food," he explained bravely. "You know, sausages and eggs and cans of beans . . ." But his voice trailed off into silence as Tilly drifted out of the room.

"She wasn't listening," said Ant quietly. "She didn't hear a word."

"No," said Perry.

The afternoon was spent as the morning had been, carrying out plans made the previous day. The tumbled outbuildings behind the house held an abundance of junk of all descriptions. From the remains of a garden gate and several blue-and-orange fertilizer bags, Perry constructed a sled of such astonishing swiftness and brilliance that its designer, at least, thought it well worth all the trouble and anxiety of the past few days.

"I don't," said Ant, who was getting tired of clambering out of snowdrifts. "I'd rather be at home doing ordinary things."

"We'd be at school if we were at home," pointed out Perry.

"I'd *much* rather be at school," said Ant stubbornly. "I *like* school. Here's Tilly coming out. I'm going in to get warm."

"Wasted on her!" exclaimed Perry crossly and out loud. "Rather be at school! And now she's cleared off and I'm going to be stuck with that silly old—"

"That is fit for a queen!" called Tilly, gazing admiringly at the sled from the top of the slope. "Fit for a queen! Proper clever that is!" and to Perry's utter astonishment, accepted with delight his offer of a ride down the hill.

"Whoever would have thought it!" she said, beaming proudly at him as he towed her back up the slope again. "Beautiful as the day! Whoever would have thought those sacks would tie on so slippy!"

Perry grinned over his shoulder at her. There she sat, tea cozy hat, legs like black sticks in chopped-off rubber boots, dandelion clock hair, a disintegrating parcel of clothes. There she sat, shining with pleasure.

"Have another go," suggested Perry, forgiving her everything, even the porridge, and Tilly said she didn't mind if she did.

It was while they were on their third descent, Tilly on the sled and Perry galloping behind, that the first snowball shot over their heads.

It was followed by a second one that caught Perry hard on the throat. He doubled up, choking, and straightened to find Tilly wiping snow from her eyes and the chip shop boy (who appeared to have acquired a double) in stitches of laughter.

In Perry's world snowballs had always been scooped-up handfuls that disintegrated on impact, but these were different. These were hard—molded round and round by leather gloves until they were heavy and half ice—and they hurt. Another flew between himself and the sled and a fifth caught Tilly on the side of the head. Perry saw her hand go up and her uncertain smile, like someone who smiles at a joke they have not understood. The way Sun Dance smiled, far too often, in the moments before he made a complete fool of himself. The moments that Perry was always trying to prevent, that inevitably ended with goading and taunts, blind rage or tears from Sun Dance, and shame for Perry.

"Look at her laughing!" said the chip shop boy. "Silly old—" and then Perry went madder than Sun Dance had ever done, even at his most embarrassing worst. Before the chip shop boy could finish the sentence, Perry had charged down the hill and landed fair and square on his stomach.

"Ugh!" said the chip shop boy, collapsing as if he had been punctured and displaying his latest installment of chips on the snow. A moment later Perry was seized from behind by the chip shop boy's double, and the fight became very one sided and would have finished quite early if Perry had not been filled with bloodred rage that kept him staggering up for more, even when pounded and gasping and with his face rubbed raw with frozen snow.

"Off his head!" panted the chip shop boy's double as Perry lurched to his feet and plunged at him again.

Months of piled-up anger were breaking like storm clouds inside Perry. Last night in the chip shop he had been intimidated; he had cared what they thought, and they were nothing. They were bullies. Rubbish, like the people who sneered at his brother. Cowards. Like himself, making Sun Dance miserable over a pile of Christmas cards. As if it had mattered. As if anyone worth a second thought had cared. Robin and Dan hadn't. *I did though*, thought Perry in disgust, and sailed joyfully back into battle.

The chip shop boy heaved himself groaning to his feet, emptied out a bit more of his lunch, and said, "Let's get out of here!"

"Cowards! Pigs!" shrieked Perry, running after them as they set off down the hill. "Come back and fight! Come back . . ." He fell over and groveled and pulled himself up. ". . . and I'll kill you! Come here . . . ," yelled Perry, the blood pounding gloriously in his head as he staggered into a stone wall. "Come back here and I'll show you who's mad!" and he sat down very suddenly and closed his eyes, and the snow was so warm and comfortable he could almost have gone to sleep.

When he looked again, the hillside was empty, except for Tilly struggling awkwardly toward him.

"Beautiful as the day," said Tilly, laying a tiny hand on his arm. "Fit for a queen!" and Perry, blinking and bemused in the battle-stained snow, knew that this time she was not referring to the sled.

"What have you done to your face?" asked Ant the minute Perry came through the door.

"Fell in the snow," said Perry cheerfully. He was feeling extraordinarily cheerful altogether. "Fell in the snow!" he repeated, glancing across at Tilly.

"I shall give you the parrot," said Tilly.

"What!"

"I should like to know he was with you. I should like to know he was safe. This time tomorrow, where shall you be?"

"Well, here I suppose," said Perry, somewhat taken aback. "I hope you don't mind."

"Not at all," said Tilly graciously. "An honor. You can leave the key under the flowerpot by the back door."

"Leave the key?"

"The gray cat is missing. I am going to look for her."

"Shall we come and help?"

"If you have never cooked, there are instructions on the porridge box," said Tilly, smiling lovingly at Perry as she left the room.

"What does she mean?" wondered Ant, staring after her. "Perry, she's much, much—"

"She's worried about her cat, that's all," interrupted Perry.

". . . madder—"

"Just because she's different! So are lots of people! Look at Sun Dance!"

"She's not a bit like Sun Dance!" protested Ant.

"She enjoyed the sled! She went down as fast as we ever did! Good old Tilly!"

"And that's not even her name!"

"Well, Sun Dance isn't Sun Dance's name," pointed out Perry irritatingly. "And Beany isn't Beany's! And Old Blanket wasn't Old Blanket's! I like Tilly!"

"What are you going to do with the parrot?"

"I shall think of something," said Perry.

six
· · · · ·

While Perry was sitting bemused but victorious in bloody snow (all blood unfortunately contributed by the hero of the fight), Beany was listening to Mrs. Brogan's second amazing installment of the story of the dolphin sword.

How astonishing, thought Beany, that it should have been found by someone so like herself. A girl almost exactly as old, someone from Porridge Hall, and someone with sense enough to keep the discovery secret. It seemed almost too good to be true. At the end of the story, Beany went upstairs to think it out, and she was there for so long that Mrs. Brogan started to worry and called up to ask, "All right, Beany?"

"Quite all right," replied Beany. "Wondering something, that's all."

"Wouldn't you be better down here by the fire?"

"No, thank you," replied Beany politely, so Mrs. Brogan laughed and left her alone, and Beany crawled back into the tent she had made out of her quilt and continued her thinking.

Where in the long-ago world of Mrs. Brogan's great-grandmother had the dolphin sword been hidden?

If it was me, thought Beany, *where would I put it? Would I bury it like treasure?* Almost immediately Beany discarded this idea. It would be hard to bury a Viking sword without being noticed, and most unhandy in an emergency to have to secretly dig it up.

Not buried, then, decided Beany.

There were caves in the cliffs just along the coast that would make excellent hiding places for all sorts of secrets, but Beany (being only eight and a half) was not allowed to visit them alone, and she did not suppose the parents of Mrs. Brogan's great-grandmother would have been any more reasonable.

Well then, not in the caves.

There is nowhere else that I can think of, thought Beany.

Perhaps that meant there had been nowhere that Mrs. Brogan's great-grandmother could think of either.

So it must be in Porridge Hall, concluded Beany, *and wherever it had been hidden, it must still be there, because nobody had ever found it.*

Beany gloated over that happy thought until overtaken by a slightly less cheerful one: *What about when Mrs. Brogan's great-grandmother grew up and left home? Did she leave the sword behind, or take it with her? Surely no one could bring themselves to part with a magic Viking sword. Was that the reason why it had never been found?*

"Mrs. Brogan," called Beany over the banisters. "Where did she go to live when she grew up?"

"What?" asked Mrs. Brogan. "Who? Where did who live? Have you seen Sun Dance?"

Beany pointed silently to the closed door of the cupboard under the stairs. "Sulking!" she whispered, and added aloud, "Your great-grandmother. Did she go to live somewhere else when she grew up, or did she always stay here?"

"She stayed here," said Mrs. Brogan, nodding significantly at the cupboard door to show that she had understood Beany's signals. "Yes, Porridge Hall became her house. My grandfather was born here."

"So she lived here always and always?"

"As far as I know. And after her time it was passed on to my father, and then it became mine. Half mine, I should say. It had been divided by the time it came to me."

"Did you mind?" asked Beany anxiously, and Mrs. Brogan smiled, remembering how much she had minded at the time.

"It was the only way we could manage to stay. Have you finished your thinking yet?"

"No, no!"

"Well, if you come across Sun Dance," Mrs. Brogan addressed the cupboard door, "tell him I'd be very pleased to see him! It's getting lonely down here!"

Beany went back to her thinking and thought: *Mrs. Brogan's great-grandmother would have needed a very secret place.*

More secret than the cupboards under the stairs. More secret than the space by the hot water tank, where Beany herself liked to hide in moments of crisis. More secret than the coal cellar, which now held the central heating boilers and, on the Robinson side, several dozen pairs of half-worn rubber boots. Perry and Ant occasionally lurked among the boots and would certainly have spotted any Viking swords lying about.

Nobody would hide anything up chimneys because chimneys need sweeping. Nor in the cupboards (far too public) and not under floorboards either, Beany hoped, because it would be terribly difficult, excavating under the carpets without being noticed . . .

There was a noise in the room.

Beany sat up suddenly and tugged away her quilt. There were strange sounds coming from somewhere. Scratchings and scufflings . . .

"Beany!" called a faraway voice, and then there was knocking. Hard knocking, from straight overhead.

Thoughts raced through her mind like leaves in a gale. She had asked too many questions, she had wondered too much, and here was the answer. Mrs. Brogan's great-grandmother's ghost! So much for dolphin luck! Beany screwed shut her eyes and dived for cover under the quilt.

"Beany!" repeated the voice. "Beany! Are you there? What are you doing?"

Mrs. Brogan's great-grandmother (if it was Mrs. Brogan's great-grandmother) sounded a little anxious.

"*Beany!* I'm stuck!"

Beany, thinking this was a most unusual ghostly complaint, pushed out her head and asked, "What?"

"Stuck," said the voice crossly and sounding most unghostlike. "I kicked over the chair that I climbed up with, and it's too far to jump . . ."

"Sun Dance!" exclaimed Beany.

"You'll need to go into my bedroom," ordered Sun Dance. "I've had to crawl over the rafters to get above yours. I thought I'd never make you hear. It's jolly dangerous up here too, and I can't turn round without going onto the ceiling plaster . . . I shall have to go back backward . . . Oh! Hello!"

Beany reached his bedroom door just as Sun Dance's face, very dusty and triumphant, appeared in the black square that had opened in the corner of his and Perry's bedroom ceiling.

"You're in the attic!" exclaimed Beany.

"Yes, and it's brilliant up here! It must be the only bit of Porridge Hall that hasn't been divided! You can get into our half as easy as anything. Come and see!"

"I couldn't reach. How did you?"

"Climbed onto the back of that chair and jumped and swung myself. That's when it fell over. Can you move it out of the way and push my bed underneath instead?"

"I think so, but . . ."

"Well, hurry up! Yes, like that! That's just right! Now climb up and take these off me! Mind your head!"

Beany ducked just in time as their mother's kitchen ladder suddenly appeared in the hole.

"Sun Dance! What are you going to do with them? If Mrs. Brogan finds out you've been up there . . ."

"There's ways down into the house all over the attic. Trapdoors in the ceilings. There's even one in Perry and my bedroom that I've never noticed before. I've pushed our bunk bed right underneath. We can get in and out dead easy! We should have done it ages ago!"

"But I'm sure Mrs. Brogan will be furious!"

"People often *are* furious," said Sun Dance realistically. "And anyway, it's for a good cause. She would be very upset if we were burgled! And I've found a cricket ball."

"A cricket ball?"

"Very dusty. It must have been up here for years and years."

It was the cricket ball that persuaded Beany, although she could never have told anyone why.

"There are paths," said Beany gazing around at the dusty attic landscape. "Wooden paths, leading all over the underneath of the roof."

"I know," said Sun Dance as smugly as if he had made them himself, "but you still haven't seen how good it is. Come over here!"

He led the way along one of the wooden walkways that crossed the attic, pointed downward, and suddenly Beany found herself looking into her own home. It was a most surprising view. There beneath her was Perry and Sun Dance's bedroom with their bunk bed pushed directly underneath the hole. Nothing, as Sun Dance pointed out, could be more convenient.

The attic was an eerie place. Cobweb-coated windows at either end let in enough light to show the positions of more trapdoors, two huge water tanks, and the cavernlike underside of the roof. Planks had been laid to allow access to the water tanks and trapdoors, but between there was nothing but wooden joists and dirty plaster.

"That's where I went to knock on your ceiling," said

Sun Dance, pointing, and Beany saw a line of wavering scuffles where the gray dust had been disturbed.

"Really difficult," continued Sun Dance, "crawling along those bits of wood. I didn't want to fall through the ceiling. No wonder they made all those paths."

"How many trapdoors are there?" asked Beany.

"Four. Two each side, but two of them only open into the bathrooms, so they're not much use—no way of climbing up to them without being noticed. I found the cricket ball near one of the bathroom trapdoors. I'm saving it for Robin; he likes cricket."

"Good," said Beany vaguely.

"It's probably antique."

"Probably," said Beany, not listening.

"So are you coming burglar trapping with me, then?"

"No. I can't. There's something private I want to do."

"Private from *me?*" asked Sun Dance in disbelief.

"Private from everyone."

"After I showed you how to get up here, you're not coming to help me?"

"No," said Beany simply.

Sun Dance, very hurt and indignant, said in that case he hoped she would fall through the ceiling and added that she need not expect any share of any burglars he caught. He dropped onto his bunk bed still huffing and puffing with indignation. Beany hardly noticed him go.

The moment she had entered the attic she was convinced she would find the sword there; and as soon as she was left alone, she crawled to the darkest, emptiest corner of the whole place, to a part where the roof was so low that anybody much older than eight and a half would have had to crawl in on their stomach to fit underneath.

Having reached her goal, Beany paused to consider. Except for the removal of the staircase, the attic must have changed hardly at all since the sword had been hidden. The best hiding place then would still be the best hiding place now. The only real difference was Beany herself.

If I was her, thought Beany, *how would I . . . ? Where would I . . . ? Oh!*

She jumped and gave a small squeal as a large black spider scuttled across her knee.

Mrs. Brogan's great-grandmother would have been wearing a dress, Beany realized suddenly. *At least I've got jeans! Imagine crawling right across here in a dress! I wonder if she managed like I do.*

Beany had long ago perfected the art of crawling in skirts, the hem of her skirt held in her teeth. The thought that Mrs. Brogan's great grandmother might perhaps have done the same gave her courage to brave the spiders. But thank goodness for jeans. She began her search, groping into the black shadows between the wooden joists, stretching on her stomach to reach under the eaves, trying to ignore her aching knees and the sticky softness of cobwebs on her fingers. She was not even very sure that she knew exactly what she was looking for. She had seen swords on television and in pictures, but that was all. It might turn out to be entirely different from any of them. Beany had thought she had known what an elephant looked like until taken to the zoo and confronted with the real thing. Perhaps the dolphin sword would be just as surprising.

Something tickled the back of her neck. Beany suddenly sat up and bumped her head. "Ow!"

Reaching up to rub the bump, her fingers encountered a dangling string.

Beany's heart gave a great leap of excitement as she craned back to see. In the gray shadows above her head, a bulky package had been stowed away, long and flat and, like the elephant, at least twice as big as Beany had expected it to be.

It had been wrapped around with paper and string and pushed behind two of the rafters of the roof. In all the years that it had been there, the weight of the roof had settled around it so that now it was trapped. Even by pushing with all her strength, Beany could not move it by the smallest amount.

For a while she sat and wondered what to do, and then she began picking away the paper that covered one end; and after a little while she was almost sure that she felt with her fingers the outline of a dolphin.

It seemed to be shaped into a leaping curve that covered the length of the hilt. In the darkness Beany traced with her fingers the smile on its face.

"*Now everything will be all right,*" thought Beany.

The attic was full of noise. The water tanks plinked and spluttered. The tiles hummed beneath the wind. The rafters settled and creaked. Footsteps sounded and Sun Dance called, "Beany!"

Beany left her dreaming and realized that any moment her secret would be out. She had wasted time; she ought to have begun wishing as soon as she had found the sword. Later, she promised herself, she would come back and do it properly, but right now there was one wish that would not wait. Closing her eyes and holding the dolphin as tightly as she could, she wished her most urgent wish.

"Mum to be better."

"I thought you must have gone," said Sun Dance, popping up into the attic just as Beany, scurrying hastily back across the rafters, arrived at his trapdoor. "Fancy having secrets and not telling me! Do you want to know what I've been doing?"

"Yes," said Beany.

"Well, I'm not telling you then," said Sun Dance triumphantly. "And it's a brilliant one! The best yet! Hey, listen! Listen!"

"I thought you weren't telling . . ." began Beany, and then heard it too.

It was the telephone, ringing far away in Mrs. Brogan's hall.

"But it's broken!" said Beany in surprise.

"It must have been mended," said Sun Dance. "Quick, Beany, it might be Perry and Ant. We don't want Mrs. Brogan up here looking for us."

A moment later he and Beany were out of the attic, the trapdoor was closed, the kitchen ladder stowed out of sight, and Sun Dance's bed pushed back against the wall.

"Beany!" called Mrs. Brogan. "Beany! Sun Dance! Hurry!"

So that is how quickly it works, thought Beany during the happy rejoicing that followed. Two minutes after she had wished her wish, there was the disconnected telephone miraculously repaired and her mother on the end of the line announcing that she was already completely better.

"Just like magic!" Sun Dance said cheerfully. "The telephone being broken and then not being broken and suddenly there was Mum!"

"Very like magic!" agreed Mrs. Brogan. "I didn't even notice them repairing the line."

Proper magic! thought Beany with awe. *Dolphin luck! But it really will have to be secret.*

It was a pity, but it was true. There was nothing Beany would have enjoyed more than escorting her friends and relations up to the attic to have their wishes granted, but what would be the result in the end if she did? Would the dolphin sword be allowed to remain where it had been safe for so long? Beany thought not. Mrs. Brogan's words came back to her: ". . . sold or sent to a museum. Something sensible and boring like that."

It did not bear thinking of.

I will have to wish their wishes for them, thought Beany.

It was a tremendous relief to Mrs. Brogan to have the telephone working again, and she immediately set about renewing contact with the outside world. She telephoned Dan's house to speak to Robin, the electricity board to find out whether the power was at last on for good, the weather station to find out the long-term weather forecast, and several friends, who were very relieved to hear that Porridge Hall had not, as they had feared, been finally blown away. Over and over again she tried to reach Perry and Ant in

Hemingford North, but although a telephone at the other end rang and rang, there was never any reply.

Beany spent the next hour or so writing a list of wishes to wish on the dolphin sword, and Sun Dance, very cross because she wouldn't tell him what she was doing, spent the time dropping enormous hints about his own private secret, so that it became less and less private by the minute.

"Don't you want to know what I was doing all that time I was in our house?" he demanded.

"Yes, please," said Beany, not even bothering to look up, and writing

VERY IMPORTANT: OLD BLANKET GONE TO HEAVEN

Ant, she remembered, had been quite desperate to be sure that Old Blanket had gone to heaven, but did dogs have such good fortune? Did anyone for that matter? Perry had said there was one way to find out. *What was Sun Dance talking about now?*

"It's not just catching them," he was explaining."It's keeping them. Perry and Ant won't be home for ages. If you want to keep them for quite a long time, it's no good at all in a bedroom."

Burglars again, thought Beany, and returned to her list.

ANOTHER DOG PLEASE

she wrote.

"You're not listening to anything I say," grumbled Sun Dance.

"I am!" contradicted Beany. "You said you've made a burglar trap, and you said it was no good keeping them in a bedroom."

"Yes, but do you know why?"

"No toilet," said Beany with horrible practicality.

Sun Dance stared at her, openmouthed with admiration, and decided then and there that his little sister was wasted every moment that she was not trapping burglars.

"However did you know?" he asked at last.

"Shut up for a minute; I'm thinking."

It was Perry's turn to have his wishes recorded, and Perry's wish had been very ambitious.

"I would wish for a million wishes," he had said, and Mrs. Brogan had remarked that such wishes were generally a bad idea—and Beany thought she was probably right. In all the stories of magic she had ever read, the extra-greedy wishes invariably backfired.

Not a million wishes then, decided Beany, *something very special instead,* and she asked Sun Dance, "Can you think of anything Perry really wants very much?"

Sun Dance stopped brooding over his little sister's uncanny understanding of the necessities of long-term burglar keeping. Years of bedtime conversations between the top and bottom bunk had left him very well informed on the subject of what his brother would really like.

"Porridge Hall to have a real ghost. His own intergalactic rocket. To find a real corpse in the garden. No relations so he could always do exactly as he liked . . ."

"Are you sure?" asked Beany, quite appalled at the thought that if Perry had chanced to come across the dolphin sword, he might well have ended up with a million such wishes all coming true.

"Especially no moaning sisters," said Sun Dance. "That's what he always says."

"The pig!"

"Tame snakes, he wants," continued Sun Dance, "boa constrictors, like the one I bought him for Christmas, not the poisonous kind, and an enormous spider like the ones you see on television. For surprising people with."

Perry, decided his horrified sister, deserved no wishes at all. "However do you know these things?"

"We talk about all sorts in bed at night," explained Sun Dance. "We used to do anyway, before he started being so ratty with me all the time. I wish he was back like he used to be! Beany, were you watching me this afternoon?"

"What? When?" asked Beany, writing:

PERRY BACK LIKE HE USED TO BE

"When I made my new burglar trap in the bathroom."

"No."

"I don't know how you guessed then."

"Easy," said Beany, and Sun Dance sighed.

"I wish I could really catch someone."

"You caught me," pointed out Beany. "And Mrs. Brogan."

"You were just practice," said Sun Dance. "A real proper burglar who isn't expecting it is what I want."

Beany thought a real proper burglar who wasn't expecting it might turn out to be more difficult to handle than Sun Dance realized, but it seemed a shame that after so much hard work, he should catch no one at all. Sun Dance should have his wish, she decided, but a real, proper burglar was going too far. She would ask for a nice, kind person instead. A nice, kind person who wasn't expecting it. It would not be quite so exciting perhaps, but much, much safer—and surely far better than no one at all.

Beany paused and chewed her pencil. There were Mrs. Brogan and Robin to be considered. She must listen for something that Robin really wanted. Mrs. Brogan, who made no secret of the fact that she was perpetually hard up, was easy. Money.

"Mrs. Brogan," said Beany, bouncing into the hall, "would a million pounds be all right?"

"I should think so," said Mrs. Brogan absentmindedly, as she dialed, for about the twentieth time that day, the number Mr. Robinson had given her in Hemingford North.

"What would you do with it?"

"Do with what?"

"A million pounds."

"Why on earth doesn't somebody answer?" Mrs. Brogan demanded, banging down the receiver. "Just listen to that rain! It must be half hail! If I had a million pounds, I would buy a villa in the south of France!"

"What!"

"You're right! Not France. Italy. Yes, Italy. On the coast."

"Move away from Porridge Hall?" exclaimed Beany, very shocked.

"They don't have winters like this in Italy," said Mrs. Brogan, as she dialed again. "I have never known such appalling weather!"

Mrs. Brogan, Beany decided resolutely, must never become a millionaire. Robin would not be at all pleased to find himself whisked off to live in Italy.

"Where *is* the dratted woman?" said Mrs. Brogan irritably.

"What dratted woman?"

"Nothing," said Mrs. Brogan, "nothing to worry about!" And then she added in spite of herself, "Oh, I *wish* the twins were safe home!"

Far away in Hemingford North, a telephone rang and rang. Nobody heard it because there was nobody in the house. Perry and Ant's godmother had made up her mind that enough was enough—she had had the most worrying twenty-four hours she could remember for years, and something must be done.

Perry and Ant, following a supper cooked after all by Tilly—it was porridge again—had gone very early to bed. They were both exhausted from their day outside, especially Perry, whose battle-fatigued yawns were of jaw-dislocating enormousness and very infectious. They fell asleep almost immediately, and minutes or hours later, Ant could not possibly have guessed which, she jumped awake and knew that something had happened.

The whiteness of the snow outside the uncurtained windows meant that it was never absolutely dark in the bedroom at night, but even if Ant had not been able to see at all, she would have known there was someone in the room. Someone stooping over the bed. Stooping low, peering into her face. Tilly.

seven

· · · · · · · · ·

Tilly by night, and even in daytime Ant had found her a half-frightening, incomprehensible person. This nighttime visitor was an unearthly creature altogether, snow-lit, oddly exultant, and strangely eerie, like a portrait in the dark.

Ant, more frightened than she had ever been in her life, dragged the covers up over her head, and Tilly carefully plucked them down again.

"There you are," she said, seeming not to hear the thunderous pounding of her listener's heart. "There you are!"

Perry! screeched Ant silently in her mind. *Perry! Wake up!*

Perry did not wake up. He had gone to bed utterly exhausted by the heroics of the afternoon, and anyway, it was a family joke what a solid sleeper Perry was.

There was nothing funny about the joke that night. Ant, alone with Tilly, had no idea what might happen next. She was rigid with terror.

Tilly was whispering something.

"I thought I'd slip away while he was asleep." She paused as if waiting for an answer, but Ant could only stare.

"I know he would say I should abide by his wishes . . ."

He? wondered Ant. *Perry? No, of course, she must mean the parrot.*

". . . but I have given him to the boy. The least I could do. A jewel of a boy. It has all worked out beautifully."

Ant groped for an answer, swallowed drily, but still could find no words.

"A shame to disturb you, but I must be off. You won't forget the parrot when you go? You won't forget him?"

Ant dumbly shook her head.

"Nor the dogs? Joseph and Mary. You're very fond of Joseph and Mary?"

"Yes," agreed Ant faintly.

Tilly nodded with satisfaction.

"Four cats there are. The gray one is back . . ."

"But where are you going?"

"Grace," murmured Tilly. "Amazing Grace."

"What?"

"How sweet the sound. I do not really care for the next line," and she recited:

> *"Patience is a virtue,*
> *Virtue is a grace,*
> *Grace is a little girl*
> *Who will not wash her face."*

Ant gave up all hope of understanding.

"A lovely night for a walk," said Tilly happily.

What was she doing? What was she doing to the bed?

"You're cold? Are you cold?"

Very, very gently, Ant was being tucked in.

"There!"

"Thank you," whispered Ant.

To her unutterable relief, Tilly seemed to have finished. She straightened up and moved quite briskly toward the door. She was going away, but for a moment she paused.

"You couldn't forget the cats?"

"No, no!" said Ant.

"There's people who don't care for them." Tilly, half over the threshold, stared back at the bed. "I like them myself. I like them, but I could never . . ."

She's leaving! thought Ant. *She's been saying good-bye!*

". . . eat a whole one," murmured Tilly, and softly closed the door.

Footsteps on the bare wooden stairs. A sleepy squawk from the parrot and a door opening. Humming in the night outside, loud and growing fainter. Ant's heart began to beat more normally and the rigid numbness in her body gradually relaxed.

"Perry!" she whispered. "Perry!" and then poked and shook and thumped him into life. "Perry!"

"Get off!" muttered Perry.

"Perry, she was in here! *Don't* go back to sleep!"

"Leave me alone!"

"Perry, Tilly's gone!"

"Tell me in the morning," murmured Perry, snuggling deeper into his pillow.

"Perry," pleaded Ant desperately. "You've got to wake up!"

"No, no," groaned Perry.

"I shall tip you on the floor if you don't!"

"Oh, all right," grumbled Perry, rolling over and rubbing his eyes. "What's all the fuss about? What's the matter?"

"Tilly was here. She came in in the dark. She stood right over the bed. I opened my eyes and there she was. She tucked me in!"

Perry began to laugh.

"She was *in* here!"

"Oh, well," said Perry yawning. "It's her house. Anyway, Mum often comes in when we're asleep . . . has a look at Sun Dance and that . . . Goo'night . . ."

"She said she was going and she's gone!"

"Well then," said Perry comfortably.

"She said not to forget the dogs. Or the parrot. Or the cats."

"Who could forget them?" asked Perry sleepily. "'Specially that parrot!"

"She said she liked cats, but she couldn't eat a whole one."

"Neither could I," agreed Perry, and despite himself gave a tiny snore.

"And she's gone and left us here! I heard her singing outside! Humming! Perry!"

But this time Perry would not wake up. He absolutely refused. He slept with his pillow pulled away and the blankets yanked off. He slept through thumps and punches. He slept when the two dogs got up in disgust and walked all over him. And in the end Ant—worn out, furious, frightened, and frustrated—fell asleep too.

* * *

94

Back at Porridge Hall, Mrs. Brogan had ordered early bed that evening, and she was relieved when nobody argued. The effects of Sun Dance's burglar trap still had not worn off; Mrs. Brogan marshaled them up and counted them: headache, exhaustion, sore eyes, sore throat. They felt exactly like the beginnings of flu.

"For really bad sore throats," Beany told her, after consulting her remedy book, "it says that you should tie a dirty stocking round your neck. It doesn't say how dirty. Do you think a sock would do instead?"

"Possibly," said Mrs. Brogan. "I've heard that remedy before. I wonder who discovered it and decided dirty worked better than clean."

"Perhaps dirty is warmer," suggested Beany.

"Very probably," agreed Mrs. Brogan. "Principles of fermentation, like a compost heap."

"Shall I go and hunt through the laundry basket, then?" offered Beany hopefully.

"I think I shall stick to aspirin and whiskey and a good night's sleep," replied Mrs. Brogan unsportingly. "I have a feeling it will work just as well, but I can't try it out until you two are safely in bed. Up you both go!"

By nine o'clock Porridge Hall was in darkness, and by half past nine Mrs. Brogan was asleep, the way through the attic had been reopened, Sun Dance had vanished, and Beany, crouched under the rafters and clutching the hilt of the dolphin sword in one hand and Mrs. Brogan's flashlight in the other, was trying her dolphin luck. She did not forget the urgent need for an improvement in the weather nor Mrs. Brogan's cold, nor her desire to have Perry and Ant safe home again, and before she left she added an extra wish for herself.

"I should like jet black hair and enormous blue eyes to make me perfectly beautiful," she said aloud. She had wanted for so long to be perfectly beautiful; it was wonderful to think it was really going to happen at last. She was just about to hurry back to her room and find a mirror when she suddenly realized how difficult it would be in the morning, explaining such a dramatic transformation without once mentioning magic swords.

"Bother!" said Beany, and rather sadly wished back her familiar brown hair and ordinary-sized eyes. For a little while she sat and wondered what to do, and then it occurred to her that she might request instead to become perfectly beautiful gradually, so that no one would notice until it was too late.

"It'll come to the same thing in the end anyway," she told herself, and went to the window to see how the weather was getting on.

A change was already in progress. The rain had stopped at last, and for the first time in days, glimpses of a starry sky were visible between the wind-driven clouds. Beany gave a small jump of satisfaction and went to bed.

Sun Dance, as soon as he judged Mrs. Brogan to be safely under the influence of her whiskey and aspirin, had wasted no time in climbing through to the Robinson side of the house. All evening he had gloated over the thought of his latest invention. It was a design so beautiful that he wondered if he might produce dozens of them as a business. He imagined an advertisement in his head:

THE HOME BURGLAR TRAP
HYGIENIC AND SECURE
FREE INSTALLATION
HIGHLY RECOMMENDED BY HIGHLY RECOMMENDED
BURGLAR TRAPPER

Now at last the snare was set and needed only one vital component to succeed. He gazed out from the landing window that overlooked the road and waited for it to arrive. The missing part was a burglar. No burglars came.

Perhaps it's too dark for them, he thought at last, and went downstairs and switched on several lights. Despite this encouragement, still no burglars came.

"Lazy things," said Sun Dance, opening the sitting-room curtains and turning on the television so that any passing housebreaker could see at a glance that the Robinsons had things worth stealing.

The house remained completely unransacked. Sun Dance, after all the trouble he had taken, could hardly believe his bad luck.

Grumbling frightfully to himself, he propped open the front door and laid a trail of piggy banks and post office savings books along the hall and to the very threshold of his snare. By now criminals should have been flocking to Porridge Hall from miles around, and yet not a single criminal flocked. Sun Dance, temporarily overwhelmed with self-pity, sat at the top of the stairs and wept. It was so terribly disappointing to be prepared for them at last and to have no one appear.

After a time Sun Dance pulled himself together, wiped his nose, got out the new vacuum cleaner, and lugged it to the porch, a free sample to any passerby.

Nothing happened.

He arranged the family's four silver christening mugs in a glimmering line across the doorstep.

Still nothing happened.

"Isn't it enough?" cried Sun Dance to the empty night, and the echo of his father's words came back into his mind: "The family silver, your mum's new vacuum cleaner. The lot!"

The lot. Sun Dance scurried back into the hall. The barometer. The doormat. Old Blanket's leash and a handful of keys, his dad's old coat, the little table with the telephone on it, the telephone directory, and the telephone itself, unplugged. Sun Dance, muttering to himself as he ran, cleared the contents of the hall and turned into the nearest doorway. The box of Christmas tree decorations—packed but still not put away—Ant's slippers, all the sofa cushions, the hearth rug, the fireguard, the clock and the pile of school reports from behind the clock, a lumpy clay bowl made by Beany and the three dried-up oranges it still contained—everything arranged in neat straight lines across the windy drive. The Lego pirate ship that Perry and he had constructed together, two years old and very dusty but still considered a work of art. Sun Dance swallowed a sob as he picked it up.

The pirate ship did the trick. A motorbike came slowly along the empty road and pulled up outside Porridge Hall.

Sun Dance, who had hurried back to his lookout at the landing window at the sound of the approaching engine, watched with beating heart as the burglar, dressed in deepest burgling black, climbed down, gave an exclamation of astonishment, and made straight for the house.

Just for a few seconds the inventor had slight misgivings about the wisdom of deliberately enticing burglars to their doom. *Was it kind*, he wondered, *and for that matter, was it safe?*

But the enormous nerve of the burglar a moment later dispelled his faint doubts.

"Hallo!" called the burglar, as confidently as any friend of the house might call. "Anybody home?"

"I can easily get back through the attic in no time," Sun Dance told himself reassuringly, and he watched with great interest as the burglar stepped into his mother's flower bed and peered through the sitting-room window.

"Casing the joint," whispered Sun Dance happily.

The burglar, having cased the joint remarkably quickly, stepped back out of the flower bed and appeared to notice the christening mug bait for the first time.

"Solid silver," muttered the burglar indignantly, "and the children are allowed to play with them!" And then there was a crash and a shriek as the victim suddenly disappeared from view.

"Fell over the vacuum cleaner," guessed Sun Dance, hugging himself in delight.

"Good grief!" moaned the burglar. "What on earth is going on? What a place to leave it! Highly dangerous. I might have broken a leg! Good Lord! Look at that!"

"Seen the piggy banks now," Sun Dance told himself, and the burglar had.

From then on Sun Dance's diabolical plot worked like a dream. The burglar (pausing only to remove a pair of very muddy boots) crossed the hall, climbed the stairs (following the trail of piggy banks and post office savings books magically as planned), and paused at the lighted bathroom. Sun Dance, to distract his victim's gaze from the trip wire across the bathroom door, had posted a notice on the medicine cabinet mirror. It read:

GOT
YOU

One step forward and one swift shove from Sun Dance leaping out of the shadows, and it was all over. In vain the burglar knocked and pleaded. Sun Dance, with the bathroom key in his pocket and triumph in his heart, took no notice at all. Wearily, but with a great feeling of peace, he went back to the garden and picked up the pirate ship.

A high tide was thumping and pouring on the beach below him, rocking through Sun Dance's mind with the rhythm of sleep as he wove to and fro between the house and the garden. The christening mugs were replaced on their shelf and the vacuum cleaner installed in its cupboard. The contents of the hall, the clock, and the cushions were all stowed away.

That's all of it, thought Sun Dance.

The front door was locked, and the lights and television switched off. The piggy banks and post office savings books were returned to their owners' bedrooms. Sun Dance climbed back through the attic and five mintues later was fast asleep.

"This is beyond belief!" said the captive, as the sound of Sun Dance's footsteps faded into silence; but being a philosophical sort of person (and luckily accustomed to hardship), the burglar, instead of breaking down in despair, drank a tooth mug of hot water, inspected the contents of the linen cupboard, arranged an assortment of towels and sleeping bags in the bottom of the bathtub, groaned, and climbed in.

"Those naughty children!" raged the burglar silently. "Those *awful* children! Far, far worse than I expected! It was all planned, I know it was!"

GOT

YOU

read the notice above the burglar's head.

"Thank goodness the taps don't drip," said the occupant of the bath.

"I suppose I have slept in worse places," said the shameless miscreant half an hour later, and, half an hour after that, "Or not slept. I shall have a terrible cramp in the morning."

Then, much later in the night, "At least I know now they're all right. They must be, to behave this badly."

That's something, thought the object of Sun Dance's ingenuity, and fell asleep.

Fresh snow had fallen during the night, not much, but enough to show a line of footprints leading across from the house and away down the hill.

"I *told* you so!" said Ant, and Perry—who from the moment he had opened his eyes that morning had insisted that Ant's story must have all been a dream—was forced to admit that she might be right.

"If they really are Tilly's footprints," he added.

"Of course they are," said Ant, and of course they were. A message in gray and white, as clear as print.

I have gone, said Tilly's footprints.

"It must have snowed a bit more after she left," said Perry as he gazed at the road, and Ant imagined the light flakes floating down on the empty hill, patterning the dark prints with a scattering of stars.

"She didn't turn back once," she said.

"No," said Perry, and loneliness broke over them like a huge black wave.

After a while they returned to the house. There were Mary and Joseph to be thought of, as well as the four nameless cats.

"And what about Samson?" wondered Ant. "He was asleep when she left. Do you think he knows?"

"He's cross about something," said Perry.

"Cross!" said Ant. "He's worse than cross!" and she was right—Samson was literally seething with rage.

"Tilly my darling!" he exclaimed furiously as Perry approached his cage. *"Tilly my darling, this is too much!"*

"I suppose he doesn't really know what he's saying," said Ant nervously.

Samson glanced at her with disgust and addressed himself to Perry.

"You *must* abide by my wishes!"

"I shan't," said Perry. "You can't boss me about like you bossed poor Tilly, but I'll get you some breakfast."

In the kitchen Ant was already busy exploring the only kitchen cupboard. It was astonishingly well organized. Cat food on the bottom shelf, dog food on the one above, human on the next and parrot at the top.

All in order of importance, thought Ant. *Samson at the top! Poor Tilly!*

The human food shelf held canned milk, porridge oats, tea, and nothing else. Perry, arriving to prepare the parrot's breakfast, stared at it in disbelief.

"I don't know why you're so surprised," remarked Ant, looking up from studying the instructions on the side of a box of porridge oats. "After all, porridge was all she ever did cook. It's a pity she hasn't a microwave . . . It would be much easier . . . That's how Mum does it at home . . . Oh, Perry!"

"What?"

"I do want to go home!"

"Five more nights," said Perry. "I wonder what dog food tastes like."

"I don't think I can bear five more nights."

"There must be a can opener . . . Yes, got one . . . Hang on!"

"If that dog food makes you sick, I don't know what I shall do."

"I shan't be. Dogs aren't . . . Uh! Absolutely terrible!"

"I know. I remember Sun Dance tasting Old Blanket's. Perry, I *can't* bear five more nights!"

"I bet cat food's even worse," continued Perry, busy with the can opener again. "Tuna and pilchard! Probably yuck! Smells worse than Friday school lunches too . . . One way to find out . . . Crikey!"

Perry dashed hastily out of the kitchen and up to the bathroom, where Ant, following after, discovered him desperately brushing his teeth.

"Awful, awful, awful!" he said, spitting and spitting.

"Perry, let's go home today!"

"What?"

"Let's go home! Let's go right now!"

"How could we? Don't be silly. What would poor Tilly think? I expect she'll be back."

"She won't," said Ant. "She won't, and I don't want her to be. You didn't see her in the night . . ."

"Oh, come on, Ant!" began Perry.

"She scared me stiff . . ."

Perry stared at his sister in astonishment. She was sounding suddenly quite frantic.

". . . I can't bear it here if she doesn't come back, and I can't bear it here if she does—"

"Yes, but even if she doesn't come back, what about the animals?" interrupted Perry. "You said you told her we'd look after them, and anyway, we couldn't just leave them."

"We could take them with us."

"Take them with us?"

"The cats can go in their boxes and the parrot in his cage, and Joseph and Mary can just come as they are. Dogs are allowed on trains. We've got enough money to pay extra if we have to."

"It would be stealing!"

"We can leave a note with our address on it. And the key under the flowerpot by the back door like she said."

"You've gone crackers!"

"We can tie up the cats' boxes and fasten them onto the sled to get them down to the station. I'll do it now, while you feed the parrot. You'd better clean him out too. There's a packet of sandpaper for the bottom of his cage beside his food. It won't take a minute to pack our rucksacks."

"Ant, we really can't go," said Perry seriously. "There's no one at home."

"There's no one here either," said Ant. "And there's Mrs. Brogan and Beany and Sun Dance and Robin at home . . . Perhaps we should telephone Mrs. Brogan . . . No, no, we shouldn't! She might say stay!" Ant gulped at the thought of being ordered to stay. "We'll just turn up. What are you doing?"

"Breakfast," said Perry.

"You can't really want porridge again!"

"I want *something!* Stir it for me while I feed the parrot . . ."

"Do you think his cage might fit in your rucksack? Wedged in the top I mean. It never would in mine, but yours is bigger. We could carry him back that way if it did."

"I suppose it might."

"We'll feed the dogs, but the cats will have to wait until we get home in case they have accidents in their boxes."

"I don't know what Mrs. Brogan is going to say."

"It's only an hour on the train if we don't keep getting off. We could be back by lunchtime."

"Lunch!" exclaimed Perry. "How long is it since we had a proper lunch?"

"One day," said Ant.

"It feels like months."

"Imagine five more then."

Perry could imagine them all too easily, and suddenly he decided that Ant was right. Of course they must go home, and the sooner the better. Tilly herself had made it perfectly clear that she expected them to leave. There was nothing else to be done.

An hour later they closed the house door. A note had been written for Tilly; the parrot (muttering hopelessly that they must abide by his wishes) was jammed into the top of Perry's rucksack; and the cats (not without enormous difficulty) were finally packed. They located the flowerpot by the back door and left the key underneath, in the company of several others in various states of rust and decay. Then they followed Tilly's footprints down the hill to the station.

That morning Sun Dance had awoken very early with the joyful feeling that something wonderful had happened. Something that mattered very much. Something about Perry. For a long time he lay in bed and wondered what it could possibly have been, and then, as the light grew stronger and the outlines in the room grew clearer, he caught sight of the trapdoor in his ceiling and everything came back to him at once. He had caught a burglar. A real, live burglar was languishing, even as he lay there, in the confines of the Robinson bathroom. It seemed too good to be true.

Then Sun Dance began to have worries. How strong was the burglar? And how strong was the bathroom door? Strong enough to keep the burglar still languishing? Sun Dance thought he really could not bear it if during the night his prisoner should have escaped.

And I forgot about food, admitted Sun Dance remorsefully as he climbed out of bed. Burglar keeping was more of a responsibility than he had expected, and a most unusual quaking feeling came over him as he assembled his mother's kitchen ladder and prepared to climb into the attic.

The feeling got worse and worse as he made his way as silently as he knew how across to the prisoner's trapdoor. It was almost overpowering as he raised it up and, on hands and knees, peered worriedly inside.

"But it's all right!" said Sun Dance, speaking out loud in his relief. There was the burglar, still safely captive, fast asleep (and snoring) in the bath.

Breakfast, thought Sun Dance, easing the trapdoor shut again. Even the most hardened criminals, he knew, when captured deserved to be fed. Sun Dance slipped back across the attic and a few minutes later was foraging in Mrs. Brogan's kitchen. Luckily there was plenty of what prisoners ate.

"And there's water in the taps," Sun Dance told himself with satisfaction.

The large brown loaf of bread hit the sleeping burglar squarely in the face.

"Plenty to last for ages!" said Sun Dance, seeing that his prisoner's eyes were open.

"Why? . . . Where? . . . What?" groaned the prisoner, flailing around in the bathtub.

"Bread and water," explained Sun Dance. "Just like the real thing!"

"Just like the real thing!" repeated the burglar. *"Bread and water!* Whatever? . . . Whoever? . . . However? . . . COME BACK AT ONCE!"

But Sun Dance, his duty done and not caring to discuss the matter, had lowered the trapdoor and tiptoed away.

eight

· · · · · · · · ·

Beany was finding that dolphin luck worked with a speed that was almost breathtaking. Even the weather seemed to be under its control. They woke up to find that the gales that had battered Porridge Hall for the last two weeks had completely died away.

"The wind must have swung right round in the night," said Mrs. Brogan at breakfast time. Mrs. Brogan, observed Beany happily, had been miraculously restored to perfect health.

"Without having to resort to the dirty stocking treatment either," Mrs. Brogan remarked. "I *knew* I didn't have the flu!"

"You had something," said Beany.

"Well then, thank you very much for curing me!"

"You mean with Dead Gran's black currant tea?"

"What did you think I meant?"

"Nothing," said Beany vaguely, and as soon as breakfast was over hurried upstairs to see how her own particular wish was getting on. Mrs. Brogan, coming in a few minutes later and finding her gazing solemnly into the mirror, surprised her very much by remarking cheerfully, "You look perfectly beautiful!"

"What, already?" exclaimed Beany. "Or are you just joking?"

"Of course I'm not!"

Beany, a little worried, inspected her reflection again.

"I look just like I always look to me," she observed eventually, half relieved and half disappointed, and Mrs. Brogan laughed.

"I came to tell you and Sun Dance to get ready for school," she told her. "There's just been a phone call to say they're up and running again . . . Oh, there you are, Sun Dance! School! Did you hear?"

"School?" asked Sun Dance, sounding very shocked. "I haven't got time to go to school!"

"And I've been trying again, but I still can't get through to Hemingford North," continued Mrs. Brogan, not noticing Sun Dance's remark. "So as soon as I've dropped you both off, I'm going to drive over and see how the twins are getting on."

"You're going all the way to Mad Aunt Mabel's?" asked Beany, pricking up her ears at this piece of news. "Won't it take ages?"

"A few hours, I suppose," agreed Mrs. Brogan. "But I expect I'll be back long before suppertime; it really depends on the state of the roads. If I'm not at the school gates when you come out this afternoon, go straight to Dan's. Robin will be there and Dan's mother is expecting you . . . Now then, Beany, don't look so excited! I know what you're going to ask and the answer is no! I'm not taking anyone with me!"

"I wasn't going to ask!" protested Beany.

"Good. I'll leave you to get changed then . . . Come down as soon as you can; I must get off soon if I'm going at all . . . It's probably not sensible, but I can't stop worrying about those two . . ." Mrs. Brogan's voice trailed away down the stairs.

"School!" said Sun Dance gloomily when they were alone. "School! How can I go to school and just leave my burg . . . !"

"Leave your *what*?" asked Beany.

"Nothing. I might tell you later. I *can't* go to school!"

"Don't then," said Beany calmly.

"What!"

"Don't then. I'm not." Beany pulled her school sweatshirt over her head. "At least, I'll go—I'll have to if Mrs. Brogan is taking us in the car—but I'm coming straight back . . . Why are you looking at me like that?"

Sun Dance was gazing at her in disbelief. Rebellion from Beany of all people! It was utterly unheard of!

"I wish you would stay too," said Beany. "I don't see how I can manage on my own."

"Manage what?" asked Sun Dance, very alarmed. This was not the usual Beany at all, and he could think of no explanation except the worst. His secret was discovered. His huge, dramatic Perry surprise was all spoiled. She had found his burglar. He could not bear it.

"How you can manage what on your own?" he asked huskily.

"You'll need your school shoes or Mrs. Brogan will notice," ordered Beany, suddenly very efficient. "They're on the landing with mine. I'll go and get them . . . There you are. It's something I've found . . ."

A tear splashed onto the bedroom carpet as Sun Dance fumbled blindly with his shoelaces.

"Something magic," continued Beany. "Proper magic."

She paused, wondering how much she dared say, half expecting Sun Dance to exclaim at once, "The sword! You've found the dolphin sword!"

"It grants wishes," she added, when no exclamations came. "It's been doing it ever since I found it!"

What is she talking about, wondered Sun Dance. Was it possible that his secret was still safe? Had she not discovered his burglar after all?

Beany, seeing his puzzled face, realized he had forgotten all about the dolphin sword.

"I've wished wishes for everyone, and they're all coming true," she told him. "It truly is real, proper magic!"

"Is that what you've been talking about all this time?" asked Sun Dance, sniffing up the last of his tears.

"Of course. Weren't you listening? Did you know your shoes are the wrong way round?"

"I'm training my feet to make do with either," said Sun Dance, airy with relief that his prisoner was still a secret. "Is that why you wanted to know what Perry used to wish for?"

"Yes. But don't worry. I didn't wish for any of the things he wanted. I've asked for something you would like though. I wished for a burglar for you! Are you pleased?"

Sun Dance was terribly tempted to reply ungratefully that he had got one already.

"I did it last night," Beany continued.

"What time last night?" asked Sun Dance, all at once very taken aback.

"Just after we went to bed," Beany told him, and Sun Dance, despite himself, was rather impressed. "What else did you wish for?"

"Lots of things. Mrs. Brogan not to have the flu. Mum to be well again, and almost straightaway she telephoned to say that she was. Better weather. Old Blanket to be gone to animal heaven like Ant kept hoping . . . That's really why I don't want to go to school today."

"Why not?"

"It's the perfect day to dig him up."

"Dig him up!"

"That's what Perry said we'd have to do. Don't you remember? To see if he had really gone to heaven. If he's still there, we'll know he hasn't; and if he isn't, then he must have gone."

"Mum and Dad will go mad if anyone digs up Old Blanket!"

"That's why he'll have to be dug up before they get back," explained Beany.

"And Mrs. Brogan won't think it's a good idea. Even Robin might make a fuss."

"Robin's at school and Mrs. Brogan is driving to Mad Aunt Mabel's to see what's happened to Perry and Ant. We couldn't have a better day to do it."

"Hurry *up*, you two!" ordered Mrs. Brogan, coming up the stairs to find them. "The car is out and I want to be off! Sun Dance, are your shoes on the right feet? They look very odd!"

"They're being trained," explained Sun Dance.

"Beyond me," remarked Mrs. Brogan, shooing them along in front of her. "I suppose they're your feet! Come on! The car's open. Hop in the back, both of you. *Not* you, Friday! You know quite well you go in the very back!"

"You will help me dig, won't you?" asked Beany privately, as Friday was stowed in his proper place.

"You know what my guinea pig was like!" said Sun Dance unenthusiastically.

"That was summer," pointed out Beany, with a look that warned Sun Dance to be careful what he said in front of Mrs. Brogan. "Boiling hot!"

"Boiling hot!" repeated Mrs. Brogan, settling in the driving seat and starting the engine. "I've almost forgotten what boiling hot feels like! Now, will one of you remember to tell Robin I've taken Friday with me if you see him before I do?"

"We will."

"Because he always hates the idea of him being alone in the house. I've been thinking, I've a good mind to bring Perry and Ant back with me if their godmother agrees. Out of sight is definitely not out of mind where those two are concerned, and they'd be much better off at school. At least I'd know where they were! It's a relief to have you two going back!"

Beany and Sun Dance glanced guiltily at each other.

"Don't forget, straight round the corner to Dan's if I'm not there at four o'clock. But I shall be back ages before that. Right, then, here we are! Whoops! Jump out quickly! Be good!"

"Thanks very much," called Beany as they waved her away. "Now quick, Sun Dance! Come on! If we don't do it now, it might be ages before we can. And the longer it is, the worse it might be!"

"It's been two weeks already," pointed out Sun Dance, "and I keep thinking about how my guinea pig's fur . . ."

"Two very cold weeks," said Beany hurriedly, not wishing to dwell on the discouraging subject of Sun Dance's guinea pig. "The worst Old Blanket'll be is wet, and, anyway, I don't think he'll be there at all. Those wishes are coming true really fast."

"It sort of melted off," persisted Sun Dance, "He was bald underneath, kind of . . ."

Beany decided it was time to talk of something else. "What if your burglar trap has caught someone already?" she asked.

Sun Dance opened his mouth and shut it again.

"You could keep an eye on it if you were helping me dig," she continued, as she walked Sun Dance very rapidly away from the school gates. "Otherwise anything might happen. They might start to escape. Fancy if they escaped before you got back!"

It was no good trying to keep anything from her, decided Sun Dance. Her instinct for anything burglarous was astonishing. "Promise to keep an enormous secret?" he asked, jogging to keep up with her.

"What? Do you think you could walk faster if your shoes were on the right feet?"

"No. Slower probably. Listen. I'm trying to tell you something. I've got one already."

"One what?"

"A burglar!"

"Not a real burglar?" asked Beany, standing stock-still in surprise.

"Yes!"

"Where?"

"In the bathroom."

"In the bathroom?"

"In the bathtub actually. Ever since last night."

"That's another wish come true then," said Beany, "What sort of burglar? Tame or wild?"

"Oh, tamish," said Sun Dance airily.

"I asked for tame," said Beany with satisfaction. "Can I have a look before we start digging?"

"Of course," said Sun Dance.

It had been hard work getting to the station. Ant had held Mary and Joseph on binder twine leashes with one hand and steadied the sled with the other, while Perry—as well as helping with the sled (which was mainly a matter of leaning backward to prevent it hurtling downhill under its weight of cats)—had managed the parrot. Packing the parrot had been quite a problem.

"They come from hot countries," Ant had pointed out. "He ought to be well wrapped up."

"How could anyone wrap up a parrot?" asked Perry. "Unless you could sort of bandage him up in a scarf . . ."

Just try it! said Samson's cold and furious eye.

"But I'm not going to!"

"I know what we can do!" said Ant, "We'll wrap up his cage. That will keep the wind off at least. I'll pull my spare sweater over it, and it can go in the top of your rucksack."

The size of the cage alone, rammed into the top of the rucksack, caused Perry to feel like he was wearing a strait-jacket, and it was made ten times more uncomfortable still by the way Samson marched backward and foward along his perch. Nevertheless they made quite steady progress down the hill until Perry caught sight of the chip shop boy and simultaneously remembered several things he wished he had made clearer the previous afternoon. All at once Ant found herself taking the whole weight of the sled alone, Samson was dumped unceremoniously in the snow, and Perry took off down the hill bellowing terrible war cries.

"Come back!" shrieked Ant, who had extracted enough of the story of the fight in the snow to understand that her brother, whether he knew it or not, had been thoroughly outclassed. "Come back! Come back!"

"Come back! Come back!" yelled Perry to his quarry far down the hill, but the chip shop boy seemed not to wish to talk; he jumped a gate and disappeared from view long before Perry could get anywhere near him.

Perry has changed, thought Ant, as her brother, red faced and breathless, trudged back up the hill. *He's gone back to like he used to be.*

"Run off again," remarked Perry as he hoisted Samson onto his shoulders.

"I saw. He couldn't be bothered to fight you. What was he shouting?"

"'Barmy. Cracked. Brain-dead.' That sort of thing. I didn't want to fight; I only wanted to talk."

"Never mind."

116

"I don't."

"Sun Dance does."

"When people call him barmy, cracked, brain-dead?"

"No. When they won't listen."

"It'll be brilliant to see them all again," remarked Perry after a moment's silence. "It feels like we've been away for months."

"We'll be home by lunchtime," said Ant.

A cheerfulness settled over them both after that. It continued right to the final bit of the journey where passing traffic had melted the snow and they each had to pick up an end of the sled and carry it. It persisted even when they arrived at the station and found themselves confronted by the same guard.

"Perhaps he won't recognize us," said Ant hopefully.

The guard, however, had recognized them already, and was staring in surprise at Joseph and Mary, the bulging rucksacks, and the laden sled that they dragged across the platform to his feet.

"You two again!" he exclaimed. "I haven't forgot! By rights I should have reported you!"

"We're terribly sorry," said Ant.

"Sorry is what you would have been if you'd slipped when you jumped off and gone under the wheels. Not to mention your nerve!"

"That was me, nothing to do with Ant," put in Perry, "and I didn't mean it!"

"You've been in the wars since I saw you last!"

"Only a snow fight," said Perry.

"Who won?"

"I did. I think I did anyway."

"Who ran off?"

"Them," said Perry certainly.

"Well," said the guard, as he loaded mailbags. "That's something I suppose. I take it you two were responsible for that creation at Castle?"

"What?"

"Looks proper horrible when the light is fading. Ghostly. You needn't say a word! You've guilt written all over your faces!"

Perry and Ant grinned self-consciously at each other.

"I was a bit of a lad myself as a boy," remarked the guard, all at once completely friendly. "You're not planning on getting on with those dogs, are you? And what's that contraption?"

"Only our sled," Perry replied. "Can we put it in your compartment, do you think? It's a bit heavy . . ."

"Them dogs can tie up in there too," the guard told them as he took the hint and jumped down to relieve Ant of her end of the sled. "They're not fit for the carriages, slathered up to their middles like that. You'd better get them fastened before we get going. What the heck have you got in them boxes?"

"Cats," Ant told him humbly as she tied Joseph and Mary to a bar inside the compartment and the train started with a jerk. "Perry! Are you all right? Have you hurt yourself?"

Perry, who had been caught off balance and thrown to his knees, struggled to free himself from his jacket.

"Not hurt," he gasped, "but there's something wet running down my neck!"

"It's only Samson's water," said Ant a moment later,

and Perry, who had suddenly found himself wondering whether parrot's blood would feel hot or cold, sighed with relief.

"Hold still and I'll get the rucksack off," ordered Ant, still peering down the neck of the parrot's sweater. "That will be easiest. Yes, his water is all spilled. We were stupid. We should have taken it out. Oh, look at him! Poor Samson!"

Samson, his cage uncovered and finding himself in a completely alien, joggling world, was for once completely lost for words. He stared speechlessly out at them, his feathers disheveled, his beak half open, and a maniacal look in his eyes.

"A parrot?" asked the guard incredulously.

"Yes."

"And cats in the boxes?"

"Our godmother's," explained Ant. "We've been staying with her. Samson is her parrot really, and so are the dogs. Only she seems to have given them to us, so we're taking them home."

"And where is home?"

"Eastcliffe."

"Got tickets?"

"Oh, yes." Perry hurriedly pulled them out. "But only for us, not for the dogs or the cats. How much . . . ?"

"Free," said the guard. "If well behaved and accompanied by a responsible owner. And I must say that in nearly thirty years on the railways I've never seen the like!"

"The dogs will be very well behaved," said Ant pleadingly.

"I daresay!"

"And Perry and I *are* responsible!"

"Are you now?" asked the guard, and he looked extremely doubtful. "Well, whether or not, I shall have to be getting on. Don't you get up to any monkey tricks when we pull up, and I should like your names and address just in case."

Meekly they repeated their names and address while he wrote them down.

"Any proof?" he asked, and they rummaged through their pockets and found their library cards and Perry's old bus pass.

"Right then," he said as he prepared to leave them. "That'll have to be that. I don't know what your parents are thinking of though. Nor that godmother."

"He's nice really," said Ant when he had gone.

"Very careful," said Perry.

"He had to ask."

"I suppose he did," agreed Perry. "Help me tie up these cat boxes again, Ant. The strings have gotten much looser since we started out."

Retying the boxes took several minutes. It was not until the train started to slow down for a second time that they realized how far they had come.

"Perry! Quick, look!" exclaimed Ant, and Perry looked up just as a familiar white figure flashed past the small window of the guard's compartment.

"Snow Aunt Mabel," said Ant.

The guard did not return until they were ten minutes from Eastcliffe, and by then the parrot had found his voice again and prolonged conversation was impossible.

"Never cared for them myself," remarked the guard

after being told several times (and very high-handedly) what the parrot considered he ought to do. "No heart to them. Nor cats, for that matter, but I must say I've never seen a nicer pair of dogs."

"They've been so good," agreed Ant proudly, and it was true. Joseph's and Mary's behavior had been impeccable. They had endured the whole journey side by side, trembling with emotion and not uttering a sound.

"Beautiful dogs!" continued the guard. "You two being met? Oy! Wake up!"

"What?" asked Perry, suddenly struck by an awful thought.

"I asked who was meeting you," said the guard. "Or is that a silly question?"

"Someone will come," said Ant optimistically. "But first we shall have to telephone home. They don't know yet that we're on this train. Hey, Perry! This is the station already! We're here!"

"No need to rush," commented the guard. "No call for you to try flinging yourselves under the wheels again! End of the line. Ten-minute turnaround, so I can give you a hand getting off. I'd like to see you met."

"It'll take more than ten minutes for anyone to get here," said Perry, and was extremely thankful that it would. The fewer people who witnessed their unexpected arrival with Samson, four cats, and two dogs, the better, as far as he was concerned.

"We'll be quite all right," he reassured the guard. "Thanks very much for helping us."

"Are you sure?" asked the guard doubtfully.

"Perfectly," said Ant, hugging Mary. "Perfectly, perfectly! And we're really, really home!"

They were home but not home. Nobody answered at Porridge Hall. Mrs. Brogan was miles away in Hemingford North. Sun Dance and Beany (who should have been at school) were horribly engaged in the garden, and the burglar (who in any case was too far away to hear the phone) was seated uncomfortably on the side of the bath consuming bread and water and thinking desperate thoughts.

"There's nobody answering," said Perry, rejoining Ant from the telephone booth. "It's ringing and ringing, but nobody picks it up. I suppose we ought to get a taxi."

"How *do* you get a taxi?" asked Ant. "We never have. I don't know if one would take us, and even if they did, it would be so complicated. Like explaining to the guard all over again. Let's just walk."

"No snow," said Perry. "I only just realized as the train started to pull in. There's no snow here, so the sled is no good, and how else can we shift all these cats? It's more than a mile. Nearer two."

It was then that they had their first bit of luck for days and days. Opposite the station was a small hardware shop. And outside the shop, propped upside down to keep out the weather, was a row of wheelbarrows, half price to clear.

"Half price to clear," read Perry, and they turned out their pockets and found they had enough money. The shopkeeper even oiled the wheel for them. That was how they got home. It took a long, long time.

* * *

By the time Mrs. Brogan was halfway to Hemingford North, she was beginning to wonder if she had been quite sensible in setting out at all.

Whatever are they going to think of me, she asked herself. *Coming all this way on these terrible roads! Interfering old busybody, that's what! Just because the twins didn't telephone. Typical of those two not to, after all! I don't know why I expected anything else. Still, they may have tried when the line was down. They sent the postcard. It's not as if I was even responsible for them. That's their godmother's job. Poor soul! This is going to look as if I don't trust her. It has only been two days. I am being ridiculous. Ridiculous.*

And then came the thought that kept haunting her.

But nobody answers the telephone.

"That means nothing," Mrs. Brogan told herself firmly. "Their godmother is going to think me simply officious! And so I am! I wish I had thought to bring something useful as an excuse for all this. Their rubber boots. They ought to have had rubber boots, all this snow."

And then a few miles later:

That was another skid! The roads are not half cleared, not at the corners. Ought I to turn back? She may well have taken them out for the day. Into York. To buy rubber boots. Exactly what I would do, and they could have lunch and visit the Viking Museum. They would both be interested. I am making a complete fool of myself!

With many other gloomy thoughts of this kind, Mrs. Brogan passed the journey. The signpost for Hemingford North appeared, and two minutes later she was in the village. Another five after that and she had arrived at the address given to her by Mr. Robinson for the twins' godmother's house:

The Yellow House
Sheepfold Lane
Hemingford North

As soon as she pulled up, she knew that something was horribly wrong.

"You're panicking!" said Mrs. Brogan sternly to Mrs. Brogan. "You're imagining too much! This is simply the wrong house!"

If it was the wrong house, it was very well disguised as the right one. For a start, it was painted yellow; and as if that was not enough, there was a notice on the gate in Old English lettering:

THE YELLOW HOUSE

read the notice bluntly.

Also it was on Sheepfold Lane. A passing tractor driver confirmed this fact, and above the roar of his engine explained that in Hemingford North there only *was* Sheepfold Lane. Or only that and Back Lane, which was nothing but a track. And that was all he knew, not being local but doing his year out from the university.

"Agriculture," he explained as he revved his engine in true agricultural fashion. "Finals next year. Nobody in, by the looks!"

"What?"

"Empty!" he bellowed, nodding at the house through a cloud of blue smoke, lifted his hand, and continued on his way.

"I know," said Mrs. Brogan, who had known from her first glance that the house was empty, the chimney fireless, and the windows dark. It looked completely deserted. The latest fall of snow, uncleared and untrodden, lay all about, a desolate surrounding blank.

Quite suddenly all Mrs. Brogan's thoughts concentrated into one panic-stricken yelp of *PERRY AND ANT! PERRY AND ANT!*

After a while she started back down the lane, and outside the station, half in a daze, she stopped the car and climbed out. For a long time she stood staring at the platform mailbox.

I must call the police, she decided at last, and just at that moment a train pulled up.

"You getting on here?" called the guard, and then, catching sight of her miserable face, "Everything all right?"

"I've lost two children!" blurted out Mrs. Brogan.

Mrs. Brogan drove back to Porridge Hall with her head full of very different thoughts. There had not been time for the guard to tell her much, but there had been enough for her to learn that Perry and Ant were alive and healthy, apparently well fed and cheerful, very handy with animals, and had somehow acquired a parrot. Mrs. Brogan's going-home thoughts were full of furious exclamation marks.

Worrying me out of my wits like that! Never so much as a telephone call! What their poor godmother must be thinking! Selfish, thoughtless, awful children! I was about to fetch their parents home! I would have called out the police! A nice fool I should have looked! What on earth have they been up to! Just wait till I get home!

nine

· · · · · · ·

"I've found an ear," said Beany quietly, and Sun Dance gave a squawk of dismay and scrambled hurriedly out of the grave. He was not at all enjoying the digging up of Old Blanket, and the deeper they dug, the less he found himself believing in the potency of magic wishes. For the last hour or so, only an awful sort of curiosity had kept him going at all.

"An ear," repeated Beany, very sadly. "I can't understand it."

"He *had* ears," pointed out Sun Dance.

"I was sure we wouldn't find him."

"Well, let's stop now," said Sun Dance. "He's still here, so we'll just have to fill him in. If there's an ear, there's the rest of him. He won't have vanished in bits and pieces. I knew it was no good!"

"We can't just fill him in for one ear," said Beany resolutely. "Not after all our work. Pass me that little trowel!"

Sun Dance passed her the trowel and averted his eyes as she began to dig very carefully around the damp black triangle she had just unearthed.

"After all, it's only Old Blanket," she said, scraping away, "We weren't scared of him when he was alive . . ."

"I was sometimes," said Sun Dance. "He was sometimes jolly dangerous when he was alive. That last year especially!"

"Well, he's dead now," said Beany firmly, and continued her excavation.

Sun Dance could understand why Beany did not want to give up all hope at once. They had worked so hard. They had been digging for hours, toiling away in a huge, sodden crater that centered on Old Blanket's grave, with spades and forks and trowels. They had started the minute they arrived back from school. They were both of them entirely covered in mud.

"Oh!" Beany gave a sudden shriek of delight. "It's not an ear! It's a corner of his blanket! See!"

"Are you sure?" asked Sun Dance, still carefully not looking.

"Quite sure. I can see the label a bit farther along! Please come back in and help."

"All right," agreed Sun Dance reluctantly. "But I'm stopping the second we *do* find an ear. Or anything else! We're bound to come across him soon if we've got to his blanket. He was wrapped in his blanket."

"He's not now," Beany said, as she tugged at the corner. "It's coming away too easily! I do wish Dad didn't always want everything buried so deep!"

"He always has." Sun Dance prodded cautiously with

his spade. "Ever since that squashed cat Ant found in the road got stuck in the lawn mower blades. Oh! Let me out! Let me out! I've just dug through something terrible!"

"Big?" asked Beany anxiously.

"I don't know," said Sun Dance, very green in the face and with his eyes tight shut. "It was tough and then sort of squelchy. It's stuck on my spade. I can't look."

Very gingerly Beany retrieved Sun Dance's spade and peered at the blade.

"Mars bar!" she pronounced, after a brief inspection.

"It can't be!"

"It is. Taste it yourself. It's the one I gave him out of my selection box. Don't you remember me putting it in? And look here! I've gotten up all his blanket and he's not in it."

"He must be!"

"He isn't!"

"Crikey!" said Sun Dance.

After this discovery, Beany's hopes became sky-high and there was no stopping her. Sun Dance, catching her enthusiasm, dug with almost equal excitement. Gradually Old Blanket's entire going-away outfit was arranged on the edge of the crater. It was all there: his blanket, the picnic rug, the sofa cushion, the dog biscuits and dog food and can opener.

"But no Old Blanket!" said Beany with a huge sigh of weariness and satisfaction.

For a while they rested in the mud and gloated over their hole. It was such a spectacular sight, so large and so engrossingly empty, that they could think of nothing else. A light rain began and they did not notice. Footsteps approached and they did not hear.

"What *are* you doing?" demanded a voice, and there were Perry and Ant's astonished faces peering over the top of the crater.

"You've come back!" exclaimed Beany joyfully. "I thought you would! I wished you would, and so did Mrs. Brogan! And you're just in time!"

"In time for what?" asked Perry, while Ant demanded sternly, "What are you doing to Old Blanket? Why have you dug up all his stuff? Where is he?"

"Gone," said Sun Dance, avoiding Perry's eyes.

"What do you mean, gone?"

"Gone to heaven."

"Gone to heaven! Not Old Blanket!"

"Well, he's not here," said Sun Dance defensively. "See for yourself."

Perry and Ant had spent an exhausting day and would have much preferred it to end with something less harrowing than the exhumation of a beloved corpse. They showed no enthusiasm for seeing for themselves.

"Are you sure you've dug in the right place?" asked Perry after one hurried glance.

"Of course we have," said Beany patiently. "We've found all his stuff. Everything, even the Mars bar. There's his blanket."

Perry picked up the blanket and shook it out as if expecting Old Blanket to drop from its muddy folds. Joseph and Mary, who had been exploring the garden, came bouncing up to investigate.

"Whose are those dogs?" asked Beany in astonishment.

"Ours," said Perry. "Tilly gave them to us. I mean

Mad Aunt Mabel but we had to call her Tilly—and anyway, she's not really mad. She named them Joseph and Mary because she found them on Christmas Eve and nobody wanted them."

"We've got four cats and a parrot as well," said Ant.

"Mad Aunt Mabel gave you four cats and a parrot!" exclaimed Beany.

"Yes, and Joseph and Mary! The parrot is really Perry's."

"A real parrot?" asked Sun Dance. "I've always wanted a parrot."

"You can share him then," said Perry. "He's in the wheelbarrow with the cats. We ought to let those poor cats out. They've been stuck in those boxes for ages . . ."

"Did you come all the way from Mad Aunt Mabel's with a wheelbarrow full of cats?"

"No, no," said Perry. "We came on the train. We only bought the wheelbarrow at the station. Is Old Blanket really not in that hole?"

"Come in and look properly," said Beany.

At Perry's suggestion the digging was continued. ("You know what Dad was like that night. We didn't see him doing it. He might just have bunged in Old Blanket at the bottom and shoved everything else on top.")

The crater, with four of them and Joseph and Mary all working at once, grew rapidly deeper. They excavated through a layer of gravel and down to the same limestone rock that made the cliffs of the coast, but no trace of Old Blanket appeared.

"It's a miracle," said Ant with tears in her eyes.

"Beany says it's magic," Sun Dance told her. "She says she's found a way of making magic wishes."

But neither Perry nor Ant took much notice of this remark, and Beany herself offered no explanation. It was enough for the others to know that Old Blanket was where they had hardly dared hope he would be, and, anyway, they soon had another distraction.

Robin arrived.

"What *are* you doing?" demanded Robin.

Sun Dance's burglar had very nearly run out of patience. All morning every creak and rustle in the roof above had stirred hopes of rescue, each time to be disappointed. The house seemed deserted. No one had come at all, not to the trapdoor in the ceiling nor to the door in the wall. Pleadings and scoldings and cries for help had gone unheeded.

The large brown loaf dropped earlier in the day on the sleeping captive's head was now more than half consumed. Many tooth mugs of water, both hot and cold, had been drunk with diminishing relish. The prospect of another night in the bathtub loomed larger and larger, and the burglar's sense of humor grew correspondingly smaller. All counting of blessings and attempts at broadmindedness ceased, and by afternoon the only thought left in the burglar's head was an overwhelming desire to escape.

There were three ways out: the trapdoor, the door, and the window. The first of these was more or less out of the question from the start. A thin and agile burglar might possibly manage to launch themselves into the air from the side of the bath, seize the edge of the trapdoor, and, clinging with their fingertips, gradually heave themselves high enough to force it open and clamber out. But Sun Dance had been lucky. His was an exceptionally stout and unathletic burglar, long past the days of gymnastics. That way there was no possibility at all of escape.

The most obvious way to freedom was by the bathroom door. In some houses this might have been feasible, but Porridge Hall was old and its doors were strong. All through the house, both doors and door frames were made of solid oak. Also they locked, not with modern sliding aluminum bolts, but with proper brass keys in keyholes. During the morning the burglar had attempted to pick the lock with the aid of a nail file and a barrette of Beany's that happened to be lying on the windowsill. The lock, however, refused to be picked, and all that resulted from desperate running charges at the door itself was a jarred neck and a bruised shoulder. Ransacking of the linen cupboard produced no spare key.

But the window opens, thought the burglar, *the top half at least!*

The window was at the side of the house, frosted glass with a pattern of ferns that the burglar had already begun to hate. Only by standing on Mrs. Robinson's ancient wicker laundry basket was it possible to see out. The laundry basket lid quickly disintegrated beneath the burglar's weight, but this did not matter very much because there was remarkably little to see: drenched fields and the burglar's equally drenched motorbike, a gray sky and an even grayer sea. Not a single person in the whole landscape.

But there are people about, thought the burglar. The back garden was out of sight, but faintly, now and then, came the voices of Sun Dance and Beany as they toiled in the mud of the open grave.

"Oy!" shouted the burglar from time to time, but no one ever replied.

"What are you doing?" demanded Robin again, staring around in amazement. "Why are Perry and Ant back home? Where did all those animals come from? Are you digging up Old Blanket? Where's Mum and Friday? Does she know what you're doing? Why are Sun Dance and Beany home from school already? I thought she told them to go to Dan's. We waited for you there. Whose is that great big motorbike?"

"What motorbike?" asked everyone, Robin having at last paused for breath.

"There's a motorbike parked round the side of your house, or there was when Dan's mum dropped me off a minute ago. What are you all doing?"

"Digging up Old Blanket," said Sun Dance, "and it's my burglar's motorbike."

"Your *what*?" asked Robin and Perry and Ant in chorus.

"My burglar. I caught a burglar last night. I'd forgotten. I was going to show Beany, but we started doing this instead."

"He's been obsessed with burglars," said Robin aside to Perry and Ant. "It's all he's talked about for days. What *is* going on?"

"They've been digging up Old Blanket," said Perry.

"What on earth for?"

"To see if he'd gone to heaven."

Robin burst out laughing.

"You may laugh," said Ant crossly, "but he's not here!"

"Of course he isn't," said Beany complacently. "I knew he wouldn't be. Come and see the parrot, Robin."

"What parrot? And you haven't told me yet where the dogs came from. And all these cats. And how did you get here? Did Mum bring you back?"

"Bring us back?"

"She was going to see you. She was really worried when you didn't telephone or anything. Whose *is* that motorbike?"

"My burglar's," repeated Sun Dance patiently.

"And the dogs and cats are what Mad Aunt Mabel gave to Perry and Ant," said Beany excitedly. "And the parrot."

"Doesn't *anyone* care about my burglar?" interrupted Sun Dance.

"Of course we do," said Robin kindly, "but is there really a parrot?"

"I made a really good burglar trap," persisted Sun Dance valiantly. "In the bathroom. A toilet you see, and plenty of water . . ."

"There really is a real parrot," said Beany. "A beauty, called Samson."

". . . and bread of course, and the bath to sleep in . . ."

"*Please* shut up a minute, Sun Dance!" begged Robin, clutching his head in despair.

"Come and look at him," urged Beany, "and you

haven't properly seen yet where Old Blanket is gone."

"Nobody ever listens to me!" grumbled Sun Dance.

"Go on then," said Perry, remembering his conversation with Ant earlier that day. "I'm listening. You think you caught a burglar?"

"I was trying to tell Robin," said Sun Dance, looking resentfully at Beany as she dragged Robin and Ant across to the parrot's cage. "I *did* catch a burglar! I made a burglar trap . . . I made four burglar traps actually . . ."

"Did any of them work?"

"They *all* worked. One caught me. One caught Mrs. Brogan. One caught Beany . . ."

"I should like to have seen them," said Perry regretfully, and Sun Dance—who had been expecting remarks such as "You must be mad!" and "You better stop doing things like that before you get to Big School!" and "If you're not careful, people will start to think you really are crackers!"—stared at his brother in astonishment.

"Perry!" called Beany across the garden. "Can we take the sweater off the parrot's cage now? It feels warmer."

"Is it a talking parrot?" asked Robin. "I always think they might as well not be parrots if they don't talk . . . I say, did you hear me when I told you Mum has driven all the way to your aunt's today? Why didn't you telephone when you got there?"

"There wasn't a phone," said Ant, horribly guilt-stricken at the thought of Mrs. Brogan's wasted journey. "We did send the postcard."

"She thought you might manage a bit more than that. She was having fits by the second day when we hadn't heard from you, wasn't she, Sun Dance?"

"Yes," agreed Sun Dance. "And she was really fed up when nobody answered when she rang. There *was* a phone. Mad Aunt Mabel called us just after you left. *Please* come and see my burglar!"

At that moment Beany tugged the parrot's cage free of Ant's jumper, and the parrot, who had been stubbornly silent ever since he arrived, enchanted them all by bursting into furious speech.

"You have gone too far!" he screeched, quivering with temper. "Tilly my darling, you MUST abide by my wishes! My wishes! My wishes! You have gone *too far!*"

"Oh!" exclaimed everyone as they crowded around the cage. "Isn't he beautiful! A real talking parrot!"

"What about a real talking burglar?" asked Sun Dance crossly, but everyone was much too engrossed in Samson to listen, and Samson, who always enjoyed an admiring audience, showed no signs of shutting up.

"Pigs!" said Sun Dance in complete disgust and marched away.

The commotion in the garden had drifted up to the burglar, and the burglar had at last decided that enough was enough. As Sun Dance climbed sulkily onto his captive's motorbike, a fat, blurry figure appeared behind the frosted ferns, there was a shout of "Stand clear!" and then suddenly broken glass was falling onto the ground below.

"Help! Help!" screeched Sun Dance, as a hand, wrapped in a bath towel and wielding the lavatory brush, whacked more broken glass to the ground. "Help! Help! Everyone! Quick! My burglar's escaping!" Everyone had already arrived. At the first crack of broken glass Samson had been forgotten and they had rushed up the garden and around the corner of the house to Sun Dance's aid. Now, in appalled silence, they watched as more and more window was jabbed to the ground.

"Do something!" wailed Sun Dance, but everyone seemed too astonished to move.

"Stand clear!" ordered the burglar, and whacked again.

"Hey, good old Sun Dance!" exclaimed Perry, causing Sun Dance to flush with happiness. "He really has caught someone!"

Yet more glass fell; the bottom half of the window was almost clear when Sun Dance, with a sudden shock, realized exactly what was happening and began to cry. His burglar was escaping. The burglar he had caught to prove to Perry that he was still Sun Dance. And the plan had worked perfectly. Here was the old Perry, reckless and tolerant, admiring his brother's ingenuity and offering a share of his parrot. He had unflinchingly admitted to pushing a wheelbarrow load of cats across town. He had called him Sun Dance.

The prisoner was making great progress with the lavatory brush. Sun Dance stopped sniffing and made up his mind.

"Now!" said the grim figure at the window, having removed the last spiky fragments from the window frame. "Who would like to tell me what utterly stupid person is responsible for this?"

Everyone instinctively turned to Sun Dance, but Sun Dance was not there; and long before he reappeared, the captive had lost her temper and shown her true burglarous colors. Her language was to the point and her opinions were not polite and nothing she said made sense. She was so utterly unreasonable that they gave up listening at all and retired to Old Blanket's grave to discuss the matter.

"I can't understand it," Beany murmured to herself. "I asked for a nice, kind burglar!"

"Are you *sure* she's not your aunt Mabel?" Robin asked the twins for about the dozenth time.

"Nothing like," said Perry.

"Well, she seems to think she is!"

"Robin," said Ant patiently. "We *lived* with Aunt Mabel! She was queer, but she wasn't like that. She wasn't wild! Just listen to her!"

"She's Sun Dance's burglar," said Perry. "The thing to do is find Sun Dance . . ."

"I'm here!" said Sun Dance, suddenly reappearing among them, "and don't worry, everything's under control!"

A demonic wail of sirens filled the air, coming closer and closer.

"I thought I'd better call the police," said Sun Dance cheerfully.

Mrs. Brogan was at last nearly home, very tired, very cross, very puzzled, but full of thankfulness that the children were safe and the worst was now over. She drove into the Eastcliffe town center and out the other side, and then slowly down the road that led to Porridge Hall. Then she suddenly began to drive very fast indeed, and as she drove she moaned, "What are they doing? Oh, what are they doing? Oh, what are they doing *now*?" because even from quite far away, she could see the flashing of blue police lights through the grayness of the January afternoon. Police lights flashing outside Porridge Hall, flashing from the tops of at least three cars, and the front of the house swarming with policemen.

Mrs. Brogan screeched to a stop, leaped out of the car, and flung herself out into a cacophony of noise. Shouting and sirens and barking and the crackle of shortwave radios, and an unearthly furious screeching: "You have gone too far!"

"Children!" screamed Mrs. Brogan, dodging the arms of a large policeman and sprinting to the back of the house. "Children! Children!"

And there they were, all five, quite happy it seemed, quite undisturbed, at the bottom of the Robinson garden.

"Nothing to worry about, madam!" said a large policeman, arriving panting onto the scene. "A slightly unstable intruder, that's all, seems to be locked in the house . . ."

"An unstable intruder!" shrieked Mrs. Brogan, immediately imagining the worst and expecting to hear the whine of bullets at any moment. "And you tell me there's nothing to worry about! Get yourselves down *at once!* Get into that hole! Into the hole! Robin! Sun Dance! All of you! Now!"

"Oh, all right," said Robin, hopping obligingly down into Old Blanket's grave, and he thought, *Poor old Mum! No good trying to explain while all this fuss is on. Sun Dance is going to catch it again!*

"Come on, Sun Dance!" he called. "Just do as she says for a minute. She's in one of her flaps, that's all."

This is fantastic! Sun Dance thought. *Just 911 and there they were, fast as magic. One day I'll be a policeman. I'd love a car with lights like that! And a siren! And those radios! And Perry's come back!* He had completely forgotten his burglar.

Perry and Ant had also obeyed Mrs. Brogan and lowered themselves into the crater, and they brought with them Samson in his cage and Joseph and Mary.

Darling Mary! Ant thought. *None of this really matters. We're home! Poor old Mrs. Brogan, I wonder where they're taking her . . .*

Perry thought, *Old Robin never gets bothered by anything. Look at him grinning away! Fancy Sun Dance calling the police! He's enjoying all this. He'd get on well with Tilly. Two of a kind! Was it those boys who snowballed her that frightened her off, or did she just go? I think she just went . . .*

All my wishes have come true, rejoiced Beany. *Mum is better and so is Mrs. Brogan. Old Blanket has gone to heaven, and Perry and Ant are back. And Perry is the same as he used to be. It is all just like I wanted.* She gazed with satisfaction at the scene around her, her mud-covered brothers and sister, the dogs and cats, the advancing policemen, the shrieking parrot, and the open grave.

Everything is back to normal at last, thought Beany. *Well, nearly normal anyway! And Sun Dance caught a burglar, and I found a magic sword!*

Normal enough, thought Beany.

ten
· · · · ·

"Sun Dance!" said Mrs. Brogan, "Give the policeman that key!"

"No," said Sun Dance. "They'll let her out."

"Sun Dance!" said Mad Aunt Mabel from the bathroom window. "*Give* the policeman that key!"

"Aha!" said Sun Dance, "You would say that! That's just the sort of thing a burglar *would* say!"

"Sun Dance," said Ant, "I think it might be Aunt Mabel!"

"You said before that it wasn't."

"That was when I hadn't seen her driving license and her passport with all the stamps on it and the photograph of us with her when we were little."

"She could have pinched those things from the real Aunt Mabel."

"Sun Dance," said Perry, "I sort of remember her face."

"Oh, all right then," said Sun Dance, and handed over the key.

* * *

Even after that, it seemed ages before Porridge Hall was finally quiet again and everyone was gathered around Mrs. Brogan's kitchen table. It was not quite the jubilant feast of reunion that Beany would have expected, considering the occasion.

"Beans on toast or cheese on toast," Mrs. Brogan had announced. "Take your pick. Personally speaking, you can starve for all I care."

"We very nearly did," said Perry, "all that porridge."

"You should have come to stay with me," said Aunt Mabel waspishly. "I'd cooked a chicken pie and toffee-baked apples. May I top up our glasses again, Kathy?"

"I'm going to open another bottle," said Mrs. Brogan. "I think we deserve it. Beany, your fingernails are still absolutely black! And next time you decide to spend the afternoon unearthing a corpse, change out of your school uniform first!"

"All right," agreed Beany placidly. "But we *didn't* unearth a corpse."

"Not for want of trying," said Mrs. Brogan, slinging plates of beans and toast around the table as she spoke. "You two can stop sniggering as well," she added to Perry and Ant. "Of all the ridiculous, stupid children, to spend two days and nights with a complete stranger . . ."

"Poor, poor Tilly," agreed Aunt Mabel. "Whatever must she have thought?"

"Do you know Tilly?" Perry and Ant spoke together.

"Of course I know Tilly. I have known her for years and so has your father. You couldn't have fallen into kinder hands! Too kind by far! People have always said she would never turn a stray cat from her door, and now I believe it. What a horrible shock she must have had, the pair of you turning up from the dark!"

"She was frightened I think," said Perry remorsefully.

"I'm not surprised."

"No." Perry, remembering the chip shop boy and his double, was not surprised either.

"She's gone away," he told Mad Aunt Mabel. "She just left in the middle of the night. Ant saw her go."

"She sneaked out while the parrot was asleep," explained Ant.

"Did she say where she was going?"

Ant shook her head. "She didn't say anything at all that made sense. She was going on about Perry and the parrot, and there was a poem. 'Patience is a virtue,' and something about grace."

"Poor woman," said Mrs. Brogan.

"No, no," said Mad Aunt Mabel, waving her glass in the air.

> "*Patience is a virtue,*
> *Virtue is a grace,*
> *Grace is a little girl*
> *Who will not wash her face!*

"Grace is Tilly's daughter. Amazing Grace! Lives in the village and runs the Women's Institute and the Parish Council and anything else she can get her hands on, including Tilly of course. I shall telephone her regarding the two dogs, four cats, and parrot."

"Why?" asked Ant with sudden suspicion.

"Don't ask silly questions," said Mrs. Brogan crossly. "Where *is* the parrot?"

"In my bedroom," Sun Dance told her. "Perry said I could put it there. We're going to teach him proper swearing instead of all that stuff he talks now!"

"There is something I would like to ask the twins," said Mad Aunt Mabel. "I can quite understand the complete witlessness that made you get off at two wrong stops, but why, when you finally arrived and found no one there to meet you, did you not simply telephone me and tell me where you were?"

"We didn't know your number."

"You could have looked it up."

"We didn't know your name."

"You didn't know my name?"

"Except Aunt Mabel of course."

"My name is Robinson! Did it never occur to you that it might be Robinson? Don't you know anything about your relations?"

"Only that you were Dad's aunt. Granddad's sister."

Aunt Mabel groaned.

"And our godmother, of course," added Ant.

"And Sun Dance's burglar," said Beany.

"Yes, and Sun Dance, *need* you have called the police when she broke that window?" asked Mrs. Brogan. "It was hardly necessary!"

"Really useful though!"

"I don't know how you make that out!"

"They knew straightaway where we could get late-night parrot food from," pointed out Sun Dance, "*and* they telephoned for someone to nail up the window, so really lucky I did call them out!"

"I am too tired to argue," said Mrs. Brogan wearily. "We shall have to get new glass in that window before your parents come back. New glass in the window, fill in that awful great hole, make some sort of arrangements for the livestock . . ."

"I think if you will lend me your telephone and directory I will call Grace at once," said Mad Aunt Mabel. "That would be one less thing to worry about, anyway."

"It's in the hall," said Mrs. Brogan. "Beany will show you . . . What's that you're looking at so carefully, Robin?"

"A cricket ball. Sun Dance gave it to me. He found it in the attic."

"Covered in dust," said Sun Dance, "by one of the bathroom trapdoors."

"Good grief." Mrs. Brogan stared at it in wonder and then took it gently in her hand. "It must have been your father's, Robin. It must be the one he cracked the bathroom ceiling with that summer he stayed here when he was eleven years old!"

"I wondered if it might be," said Robin. "Do you mind if I keep it? Or would you like it yourself?"

"Of course you can keep it," said Mrs. Brogan, handing it back at once.

"I wish I knew what had happened to his bat."

"I don't know. I remember there was talk of my father confiscating it. I don't recall now if he ever did. It was all so long ago." Mrs. Brogan, no longer fueled by anger, sighed and then looked up as Aunt Mabel returned.

"Allergic to fur and feathers!" snorted Aunt Mabel. "A likely tale! Happy her mother managed to find them a pleasant home! Glad to hear the children arrived safely and suggests they shouldn't be allowed to roam the countryside unattended in the future. Pleased to accept my apologies! Dreadful woman! No wonder Tilly escapes to her cottage on the hill."

"Is she really dreadful?" asked Perry anxiously.

"Actually," said Mad Aunt Mabel, "no. She had a perfect right to be cross. Do I hear the telephone ringing?"

"I'll get it," said Robin, glad of something to do, and returned a minute later with a grin on his face.

"Mr. Robinson," he told his mother. "Says it's very hot and they've had lunch and a swim and is everything all right. So I told him it was but that Perry and Ant were back and had been given a parrot and two dogs and some cats, and the police had gone and Aunt Mabel was here. I thought I'd get it over for you," he added as his mother and Aunt Mabel simultaneously leaped to their feet and dashed to the hall.

"What did Dad say?" asked Perry.

"'Get your mother!'" said Robin.

Aunt Mabel stayed that night in one of Mrs. Brogan's spare rooms.

"But tomorrow," she said, "I shall move in next door, the children can go back to school, and we will have a bit of peace to get things straight!"

"You are a saint!" said Mrs. Brogan.

"And I will take the cats. Old maids in cottages should keep cats, so that settles all the animals, and you can stop worrying, Perry and Ant. Your father can drive them over to me one day when he gets back."

"A saint *and* a martyr!" said Mrs. Brogan.

"Fancy Mr. Robinson agreeing to the dogs and the parrot!" remarked Robin.

"He must have had a drink," said Perry. "Still, he's done it now! Too late to change his mind!"

"I never thought he really would," admitted Ant. "I knew Mum would, but I thought he'd make an awful fuss."

"Of course he wouldn't," murmured Beany sleepily. "The animals were part of it."

"Part of what?" asked Ant. "Wake up, Beany!"

Part of the dolphin luck, thought Beany, as her head nodded forward. The lovely, lovely dolphin luck that seemed to permeate the house like sunshine.

"That child ought to be in bed," pronounced Mad Aunt Mabel. "Just look at her!"

"We all should," agreed Mrs. Brogan, getting up and hauling Beany to her feet. "Do wake up, Beany! Just till we get you upstairs! Tomorrow will be a busy day. School for this lot, and even if nothing else gets done, I will have locks on those attic doors before I'm a day older. The thought of Sun Dance prowling about on that ancient plaster frightens me to death. Locks on all four entries. Mrs. Robinson agreed when I spoke to her this evening. The whole roof needs a good going over, inside and out after all the wind we've had but that can wait a little . . . *Help* Beany on the stairs, one of you; she's wobbling all over the place!"

"Beany, wake up!" said Beany's teacher. "I never saw such a dreamer! Come and hand out these sheets of paper for me! You can all finish off the day with some drawing while I get these new books sorted out."

"What shall we draw?" asked someone, and the teacher, with Beany's dreaming face in mind, said, "Draw the thoughts that are in your head."

Beany drew a Christmas tree, blowing in the wind. She drew Old Blanket's grave. She drew a turkey and crossed it out. She drew a bed and turned it into an airplane with her mother and father on it. She drew a sword with a dolphin-shaped handle, but it didn't look like a sword. She drew Aunt Mabel's motorbike, two dogs, four cats, and a parrot. She drew a black square and wondered what it was and then thought, *A trapdoor. Open.*

Beany leaped to her feet so suddenly that everything on her desk clattered to the floor.

"I wondered when you'd wake up." The teacher laughed. "Time you were off, Beany! Everyone's gone but you! You were so engrossed . . ."

Beany tore out of the classroom, leaving paper and pencils scattered at her teacher's feet. She pushed through the cloakroom and fled across the playground. She brushed past Sun Dance and Mrs. Brogan waiting at the school gates as if they were invisible. She ran all the way home.

Do wake up, Beany . . . locks on those attic doors before I'm a day older . . . Mrs. Robinson agreed . . . The whole roof needs a good going over, inside and out . . . Wake up, Beany!

Porridge Hall at last. Beany hurled herself at the front door, found it locked, and sprinted around to the back, noticing as she passed that the bathroom window was already mended, noticing too the stout figure of Aunt Mabel at the end of the garden, raking smooth the grave.

The back door was standing open. Beany dashed inside and up to her brother's bedroom and saw on the trap-door what she had been dreading. A silver disc of metal. A lock.

There was a sudden sound of scraping wood, a stepladder being moved across the bathroom floor. Beany peered around the door. A man with his back to her had just picked up a drill. He began to whistle and did not see Beany as she silently removed the key, closed the door, and locked it from the outside.

Robin was just coming in when Beany bolted past him and around to the Brogan side of the house.

"Oy!" shouted Robin, and followed her upstairs just in time to see her clamber from her mother's kitchen ladder into the roof. "Ouch!" he exclaimed as the ladder swayed and fell on top of him. "Hey, Beany!"

They will find it and take it away, thought Beany. *I will never get another chance after this, not with all those locks on the doors.*

"You all right, Beany?" called Robin. "What are you doing? For goodness' sake be careful!"

"Robin," Beany's face, anxious and beseeching, appeared in the black hole. "Please keep everyone away for a while! Please!"

"I don't see why," began Robin, and stopped at the sound of voices from downstairs.

"Please!" begged Beany.

"Oh, all right."

"Robin!" Mrs. Brogan, gasping for breath, was calling from below. "I'm looking for Beany! Sun Dance, go next door and see if you can find her! Robin, is she here?"

"She came in a minute ago," said Robin, stalling as

best he could. "You're out of breath! Would you like a cup of tea?"

"Don't be silly! Where is she?"

"Upstairs," said Robin truthfully. "Why did you run home? Didn't you take the car?"

"Oh!" groaned Mrs. Brogan, clutching her head. "The car! Did I lock it? I hope I locked it! I left it to run after Beany. She pushed past us so quickly . . . Where *is* she, Robin?"

Beany tugged and tugged at the paper-wrapped bundle. It was finally moving, but not enough.

I shall never manage to get it out, she thought, *but still, if I wish it to be safe, safe and still here, but where no one can find it, a very last wish . . .* She tugged again. *And then at least it will still be in Porridge Hall. Somewhere close by always . . .*

I can hear Mrs. Brogan, thought Beany a moment later. *I must hurry. Robin can't keep people away forever . . . Good old Robin. I haven't wished a single wish for him though. He never said anything he wanted . . .*

"She's in the attic?" came Mrs. Brogan's voice, suddenly very close. "Robin! Why on earth didn't you tell me before that she was in the attic?"

All at once Beany knew something that Robin wanted very much indeed. He had named it only the night before, and she had seen the expression on his face.

Two last wishes then, Beany thought, grasped the hilt, shut her eyes to concentrate, and spoke them aloud.

"Beany! What do you think you're doing?" called Mrs. Brogan, sounding as if she was right underneath her.

". . . and the dolphin sword safe for ever and ever," finished Beany, and opened her eyes.

"Robin, go up to her! No, wait a moment, I'll fetch you a flashlight! Beany, stay where you are and don't move!"

"Beany!" called Robin in a low voice, "Mum's gone now. Tell me what's the matter."

"Nothing." Beany sniffed and wiped her nose on her sleeve, still clutching the hilt of the sword because she could not bear to let it go.

"Beany, nobody is cross with you," called Mrs. Brogan, returning with the flashlight. "I'm sending Robin up . . . Be careful, Robin! . . . There! . . . Can you see her? Is she all right?"

A white beam of light suddenly swung through the attic and stopped at Beany crouching under the eaves.

"She's fine," called Robin, ignoring Beany's frantic go-away gestures. "Quite all right, aren't you, Beany?"

Just at that moment there was a sound of running footsteps approaching, and then Sun Dance, hoarse with excitement.

"Mrs. Brogan," they heard, "you'll never guess what! There's another burglar locked in our bathroom! Perry said to come and get you straightaway!"

"WHAT!"

"He's making an awful noise!"

"It's not a burglar," said Mrs. Brogan, coming to her senses. "It's the man putting the locks on the attic doors."

"That's what Aunt Mabel said, but it sounds like a burglar to me and Perry. A very cross one, and Perry says he thinks he's trying to unscrew the lock, and Mad Aunt

Mabel is sitting on the stairs sort of laughing and crying and shouting, and Ant is pouring cold water on her but it isn't doing any good."

Mrs. Brogan groaned. "Robin!" she called desperately. "I've got to go next door . . ."

"I know. We heard. We're quite all right."

"Don't do anything silly! Just fetch Beany out. I'll be straight back . . . Wait, Sun Dance! Wait!"

"That's all right then," said Robin, as the voices died away. "They've gone. What is it you've got over there, Beany?"

"Nothing, nothing."

"Let me look! Gosh, this roof is low! I shall have to crawl. Is it something you've hidden?"

"No."

"I can see it now. Can't you get it out?"

"No."

"If we pull away some of the paper . . . Let me get a good hold . . . There! It's coming!"

"Oh!" wailed Beany. "Why didn't it disappear? That's what I thought it would do."

"What?"

"Magic away!"

"Of course it won't magic away! Look! I've nearly got it. Let's get the paper off. It feels like something wooden."

"It isn't."

"Hold the light a minute! I think I know what this might be! Beany! Are you crying?"

"No."

"I've got it . . . Hang on! . . . Oh, Beany! Look what you've found!"

"It's all spoiled now!"

"It's not. It isn't hurt at all. Don't you want to see it?"

Beany shrugged her shoulders, rubbed away the last of her tears, turned slowly to look, and then stared and stared.

"It's a cricket bat," she said at last, and then, "A cricket bat! Of course, it's your father's cricket bat!"

"He must have hidden it, and it's been there for all these years! Dad's old cricket bat!" Robin hugged it tightly to his chest. "What fantastic, perfect . . ."

"Magic," said Beany.

"Luck," said Robin.

Literature Circle Questions

Use the questions and activities that follow to get more out of the experience of reading *Dolphin Luck* by Hilary McKay.

1. At the beginning of the story, Mrs. Brogan tells a story about "dolphin luck." Summarize the story and explain dolphin luck.

2. Why do the Robinson children split up?

3. Perry and Ant go to stay with their Aunt Mabel who will look after them while their parents are away. How do Perry and Ant end up "looking after" Tilly?

4. When Mrs. Robinson must go away, her children act like they are glad she is leaving. Read aloud the passages that show the children don't really want her to leave.

5. Why do Beany and Sun Dance dig up Old Blanket? What explanation do they have for what they find? Is there another explanation?

6. Contrast Aunt Mabel and Tilly. Given the attitude Perry and Ant have about Aunt Mabel at the beginning of the story, how does Tilly fit their expectations?

7. Re-read the passage in which the burglar is captured. Why did Sun Dance conclude he had captured the burglar? Did this person have a reason for coming to Porridge Hall.

8. Perry and Ant run into trouble on their way to Aunt Mabel's house. What are three problems they encounter and what solutions do they find?

9. Beany's wishes seem to come true. What evidence can you find that her wishes are granted?

10. What is Beany's motive for keeping the sword secret? How would the story be different if Sun Dance or Robin had found the sword instead of Beany?

11. Authors often send characters on journeys. Compare the journey Perry and Ant take to visit their Aunt Mabel to the journey they take back to Porridge Hall.

Note: The questions are keyed to Bloom's Taxonomy: Knowledge: 1-3; Comprehension: 4-7; Application: 8-9; Analysis: 10-11; Synthesis: 12-13; Evaluation: 14-15.

12.   Perry and Ant end up at Tilly's house by mistake. How might the story have been different if Perry and Ant had stayed with Aunt Mabel?

13.   All of Beany's wishes seem to come true. She believes this is because of the magic sword. Can you propose an alternate reason that these wishes come true?

14.   There are many secrets in the story. Beany keeps the sword a secret. Sun Dance keeps the "burglar" he caught in the bathroom a secret. Mr. and Mrs. Robinson keep a secret about Old Blanket. Justify the characters' decisions to keep secrets from each other.

15.   Fairy tales often include magic and end with characters living "happily ever after." Would you consider *Dolphin Luck* to be a fairy tale? Why or why not?

Activities

1.   Hollywood has decided to make a movie version of *Dolphin Luck*. Design a poster for the movie. Choose any five characters from the story and decide who will play them in the movie. (You can choose famous actors or people you know from school.) Your poster must include a movie title; the names of five characters and the actors who play them; and an image (picture) that represents a scene, character, or object from the movie. Have fun!

2.   The characters in *Dolphin Luck* wish for many things. Imagine you can have one wish come true. Write a paragraph about how this could make your life better. Write another paragraph about how this wish could possibly cause some trouble.

HILARY MCKAY grew up as the oldest of four girls in a family devoted to books. They had no television, and an engineer father who could tell such superb stories they would be scared to go to bed. She studied biology in college until she became very tired of dissecting things and switched to English. Her books include *Dog Friday*, *The Amber Cat*, *The Exiles*, *The Exiles at Home*, and *The Exiles in Love*. She lives in England.